"Oh, *my*," Rose whispered.

Everyone else in the vicinity faded into shadow
as Duncan Burke approached. Rose could swear
she could hear a chorus singing his name in four-
part harmony. Duncan Burke. *Duncan Burke.*
DUNCAN BURKE.

It was too much. The lantern jaw, the cleft in his
chin, the black hair and dark eyes. The way one
small wave parted from the rest and caressed his
forehead. His height, his shoulders, his stomach, or
rather lack of one. The rumbling bass of his voice.

She, Rose Franklin, had found the perfect man.
There he was. The one. The one man worthy of a
certain size-eight, pearl-encrusted bridal gown with
cathedral train, slightly worn.

In fact, Rose wasn't certain if the dress was worthy
of him.

Heather Allison lives in Houston, Texas, with her electrical-engineer husband and two live-wire sons. A former music teacher who traded a piano keyboard for a computer keyboard, she enjoys researching her books and is not above involving her family. The boys suggest that future stories revolve around food, video games and extended school holidays. Heather threatens to write one about sons who do all the cooking and housework.

Books by Heather Allison

HARLEQUIN ROMANCE
3284—HAUNTED SPOUSE
3309—COUNTERFEIT COWGIRL
3341—THE SANTA SLEUTH
3386—UNDERCOVER LOVER
3421—TEMPORARY TEXAN
3445—MARRY ME

HARLEQUIN TEMPTATION
(Writing as Heather MacAllister)
543—JILT TRIP
583—BEDDED BLISS
616—CHRISTMAS MALE

His Cinderella
Bride
Heather Allison

Harlequin Books

TORONTO • NEW YORK • LONDON
AMSTERDAM • PARIS • SYDNEY • HAMBURG
STOCKHOLM • ATHENS • TOKYO • MILAN
MADRID • WARSAW • BUDAPEST • AUCKLAND

To Eleanor MacAllister, who knows what it's like to
raise MacAllister boys.

ISBN 0-373-03466-0

HIS CINDERELLA BRIDE

First North American Publication 1997.

CHAPTER ONE

"How was the wedding, Mrs. Donahue?" Rose Franklin reached for the plastic garment bag the woman clutched to her ample bodice.

"My baby looked so beautiful!" Mrs. Donahue hugged the garment bag tighter, squashing what Rose knew to be a heavily beaded bridal gown—the most expensive one of her rentals. "I knew she would. Even barefoot and without the veil, she looked stunning every time she tried on the dress. It could have been made for her."

But it hadn't been. Mrs. Donahue's daughter was the seventh woman to be married in the dress after Rose bought it from the original bride and added it to the rental stock at Rose's Attic. But Rose wasn't going to mention that to this mother of the bride.

Mrs. Donahue drew a deep breath, her gaze sweeping the crowded clothing rods that lined Rose's two-story shop. "I just wish..."

"That you could keep it?" Rose finished for her. "It's for sale," she pointed out with a sympathetic smile. But it was expensive and Rose knew the woman wouldn't buy the dress. Frankly, Rose didn't know if she could part with it.

"I know." Mrs. Donahue sighed and, to Rose's relief, relaxed her grip.

5

Although the dress was of superb quality, after each wearing Rose had to reinforce the seams in the fragile silk and rebead any noticeably bare areas before it could be cleaned and rented again.

"My daughter doesn't have a sentimental bone in her body." Mrs. Donahue at last handed the bag to Rose. "I still have my wedding gown," she added plaintively. "But of course Stephanie is so much taller than I am, she couldn't wear it."

"She'll have the veil you made for her," Rose commented as she hooked the heavy garment bag on the metal rod next to the counter. "That will make a lovely keepsake."

Mrs. Donahue brightened. "You're right, of course. And grooms have been renting their tuxedos for years," she said, parroting Rose's oft-mentioned observation.

Mrs. Donahue was like many mothers of the brides who found their way to Rose's consignment and rental shop in the Rice Village area of Houston. Some were horrified at first by the thought of their daughters renting or buying a secondhand bridal gown, but Rose handled only the most exquisite garments. Mrs. Donahue's daughter, Stephanie, had rented not only her wedding dress, but vintage dresses for her bridesmaids. The young women had been transformed into elegant characters from a fairy tale and the bride was marrying her Prince Charming.

Rose smiled wistfully, then unzipped the bag so she could inspect the dress for damage. It was a necessary but potentially awkward moment.

"So beautiful," murmured Mrs. Donahue, helping Rose peel away the garment bag.

"Yes." The faint scent of Stephanie's floral perfume still clung to the dress. As usual, makeup smudges on the shoulders were testament to the hugs the bride had received. Rose blinked, imagining Stephanie's happiness.

When the gown had first become available, Rose had kept it back, thinking she'd like to wear it for her own wedding. She never wore the clothes in her shop, but for this exquisite creation, she'd gladly make an exception.

Almost from the moment she saw it, she'd dreamed of wearing this dress while walking down the aisle of a church to meet her groom. At the time, she'd been dating the owner of the bookstore three shops down from Rose's Attic. Funny, but it was because of this dress that she'd realized she wasn't in love with Horace.

One afternoon, he'd caught her holding the gown up to herself and daydreaming at her reflection in the mirror. Horace had thought the dress was "excessive". Horace pronounced many of the clothes Rose sold at her shop "excessive". Evidence of a decadent life-style, he felt. As she'd stared at his pursed countenance that day, Rose had realized that he'd never been the groom in any of her wedding dreams.

As a groom, Horace simply couldn't do justice to the pearl-encrusted lace and cathedral train, and Rose knew she would never marry until she found a man who could.

In the meantime, other brides wore the dress to marry and Rose continued to dream.

Now, she lifted the heavy lace and beading and spread out the train. After a first glance revealed no tears or stains, she relaxed. Once more, the dress was safely back in her possession.

"Do you need help carrying in the bridesmaids' dresses?" she asked Mrs. Donahue, who was surreptitiously wiping moisture from her eyes.

With a last sniff, Mrs. Donahue nodded and preceded Rose out into the April sunshine.

"I can't figure out how Stephanie even found your shop." Mrs. Donahue opened the door of a large older-model car parked in one of the three parking spaces available in the front of Rose's Attic. "I wouldn't have driven down this street. I thought these were homes."

Rose reached into the rear seat for the rustling taffeta dresses and the cloud of net petticoats. "They used to be." And in fact, Rose lived in the back part of the old gray stone house in which her shop was located. "But now they're part of the Village." Rice Village was a lovely area of Houston, with huge old oaks and masses of blooming azaleas, though they were past the peak of their season.

"Just barely part," Mrs. Donahue said from behind the open trunk lid.

Which was why Rose could afford to lease the house. "Not really. A couple of antiques dealers, a photographer and a rare book store are with me on the block." Her arms filled with fabric, Rose bumped the car door shut with her hip. "And an interior decorator will be moving in across the street."

Mrs. Donahue slammed the trunk closed and lifted a cardboard box containing the gloves and hats the bridesmaids had worn.

"Well, your shop *is* charming," she said as Rose held the door open with her foot. "Even though it's so out of the way. You should advertise."

"Advertising is expensive." The bell clanged as Rose let the door close behind her and piled her armload onto the Victorian cut-velvet settee. "People seem to find me," she said with a touch of defensiveness, though she knew she could be doing better. She took the box from Mrs. Donahue and withdrew the rental inventory sheet. "Now, we need four pairs of gloves...four pillbox hats and four pearl chokers."

Mrs. Donahue removed the hats and their short veils first. "I remember when we all wore these. Now they're called vintage. *I* don't feel vintage!"

Rose laughed and marked them off the list, then began pairing up the gloves. "What's this?" Underneath the gloves was a brown leather book. "It's a day planner," she said, recognizing a larger, more detailed version of one she owned. "Yours?" She tried to hand it to Mrs. Donahue.

"No." Mrs. Donahue shook her head.

The planner was encased in a worn leather binder and was obviously much used. "I'll bet somebody's frantic," Rose commented, snapping it open. "I know I would be." Papers and business cards spilled out. Rose stuffed them back inside and flipped to the front. "Duncan Burke?" she questioned, reading the name off a laminated business card and notice promising a reward to anyone who found and returned the planner.

"Oh, Duncan!" Mrs. Donahue grimaced. "One of the groomsmen. He kept leaving the reception to make phone calls. I thought we'd never get him to pose for the wedding pictures."

"This business card says Burke and Bernard Advertising Agency." With an address in the expensive Galleria area.

Mrs. Donahue peered over Rose's shoulder at the card. "Alan, my new son-in-law, said Duncan was in advertising, but I didn't realize he owned his own company. He kept apologizing for the interruptions, but frankly, I just thought he was trying to impress all his friends." Mrs. Donahue reached for the planner, at the same time checking her wristwatch. "I don't know when I'll get this back to him." She sighed. "I've still got out-of-town guests. I'm meeting them for lunch, and then I've got to drive my cousin to the airport."

"Tell you what," Rose said, taking back the planner. "I'm going to the dry cleaners anyway. I can take this to him when I'm out."

"Rose, that's sweet of you, but you don't have to. I know it's out of your way."

"I don't mind." She grinned. "While I'm there, maybe he'll give me some advertising pointers." Mrs. Donahue was right. Rose did need to advertise. She had no intention of accepting the reward mentioned on the card, but did hope a grateful Mr. Burke would make a few suggestions for stretching her modest advertising budget.

"Are you sure?" Mrs. Donahue asked, her relief obvious.

Rose nodded. "It's not a problem." She set the planner aside and gestured to the box. "Now, four pairs of gloves..."

Once Mrs. Donahue departed, Rose had the shop to herself. As she reinforced the button loops near the waist of the dress, she glanced toward the door. Not a single car drove by in the two hours she fussed with the bridal gown. Perhaps it was because of Mrs. Donahue's comments and the opportunity to talk with Duncan Burke that Rose was so aware of her lack of customers. True, prom season was coming up and business should increase. Spring dances and holiday parties generated Rose's most profitable times.

As for the other times, designer suits and winter coats lined one wall. Dresses, skirts and sweaters lined another. Hats, belts and purses hung from wooden pegs. Costume jewelry gleamed in glass cases. Rose's Attic contained everything needed to outfit a woman who lived a full and exciting life.

One, in fact, that Rose wished she led.

Rose waited to leave until her assistant, Connie Byrd, arrived just before noon. Connie studied at nearby Rice University and worked at Rose's Attic part-time.

"Has it been busy today?" Connie asked. She dumped a stack of textbooks on the counter. "I've got a paper due Friday."

"It's been quiet this morning," Rose said, wishing it hadn't been. "Stephanie's mom returned the dresses and I'm headed for the cleaners."

"Do I need to do any repairs?" Connie already had her books open.

Shaking her head, Rose bundled the dresses and started toward the back of the shop. "I already did them." She loaded the dresses into her van, then returned for the bridal gown. It would have to go to a specialty cleaner, which was, naturally, more expensive. "Connie, I've also got to run out to the Galleria, so you'll be in charge all afternoon. Think you can handle it?"

Connie waved her hand. "Of course."

Rose hesitated. "Remember to fill out an inspection before the customers take the clothes."

"And have it signed. I know, I know," Connie grumbled, already flipping through her reference book. "I won't make *that* mistake again."

Rose probably shouldn't have said anything. It was true that Connie had learned her lesson, but it had been an expensive one that had resulted in the loss of an evening gown. Oh, well. Connie was a good, dependable worker. And she worked cheap.

Within an hour, Rose exited the 610 loop to the Galleria.

The noisy, shiny new Galleria area contrasted with Rose's sedate Village neighborhood. Traffic clogged the streets. People were probably returning from lunch at one of the trendy restaurants in the area, Rose thought with envy. Glancing to her left, she saw thousands of cars crowding the Galleria shopping mall parking lot. *And I can't even fill three spaces in front of my shop.*

That was going to change, she decided, turning onto Post Oak. When she refused the reward for returning his planner, Duncan Burke could hardly refuse to chat with her a few minutes, could he?

Tall office buildings encased in mirror-glass siding reflected the sun, making it difficult for Rose to see the addresses. She spotted the correct one, then had to drive past, turn around and figure out which parking garage to enter. Once she was inside, she had to drive in a tight spiral until she found a floor with space on it.

Despite her earlier high-minded resolve to refuse money, by this time Rose felt she deserved a reward. A big one.

Pulling open the building's heavy glass door, she stepped inside and searched for the directory. Her gaze encountered the well-dressed people waiting at the bank of elevators and Rose immediately wished she was wearing something other than her long denim skirt and quilted vest.

Self-consciously approaching the building directory, Rose couldn't help contrasting the other women's sleek bobs with her own windblown hair, their pumps and leather purses with her flats and cloth hobo bag.

She gazed at the planner in her hand. Though worn, it retained an air of elegance, like the clothes in her shop.

For a moment, Rose considered leaving the planner with the building receptionist, but squared her shoulders, located the office of Burke and Bernard and headed for the elevator.

She stepped off the elevator to find that Burke and Bernard apparently leased the entire floor.

An entire floor in a Galleria office building? This must be one successful agency. Feeling intimidated, Rose wiped her hands on her skirt, drew a deep breath and opened the door.

"I'm Rose Franklin. I'd like to see Duncan Burke, please," she announced before the receptionist could ask. Before she lost her nerve.

With a professional, red-lipped smile, the blond receptionist reached for an appointment calendar. "Is Mr. Burke expecting you?"

Rose watched the receptionist's manicured nail skim the appointment book. Of course, Duncan Burke was a busy man. Why hadn't Rose thought to call first?

"No, he isn't." Rose slid the planner out of the receptionist's sight. "I was in the area and hoped he might have a couple of minutes free."

"In reference to... ?"

Rose didn't want to tell the receptionist and have the woman offer to return the planner. Having battled traffic, negotiated the parking garage and left her shop in the inexperienced hands of her assistant, Rose felt entitled to a face-to-face meeting with Duncan Burke. "The, uh, Donahue wedding." It was the first thing she thought of.

"Oh, personal." Rose's explanation seemed to satisfy the receptionist, who quickly studied the appointment book. "He's with clients right now and doesn't like to be disturbed during a presentation, but he has an appointment with someone else in twenty minutes. This meeting should end soon. Would you like to wait and take a chance?"

"That's fine. Yes. I'll wait. Don't disturb him." Rose backed toward a seating area as she babbled. "Thanks."

She sank into the plush maroon seats with relief. What was she doing? She should just abandon the planner to the receptionist and scurry back to Rose's Attic.

But she didn't. And the only reason she didn't leave was because the receptionist intimidated her. If Rose left the planner with her, she had a feeling the woman would insist on taking her phone number and address. She looked like the efficient sort and they always squeezed information out of people. Rose ought to quietly leave and mail the stupid thing to Duncan Burke. Anonymously.

That's what she'd do. This man obviously was incredibly busy with massive corporate accounts. Framed print ads lining the walls of the waiting area represented important ad campaigns. Rose had heard of all of them, which said a lot about Burke and Bernard's effectiveness.

And here she was trying to chisel a few minutes of free advice from this man. She wanted to slink away in embarrassment.

She was about to, except at that precise moment, two women, dressed in just the sort of power suits Rose wished she'd worn, walked through the glass doors, nodded to the receptionist and seated themselves by the telephone. They were now between Rose and the doors.

One woman removed an earring and used a gold pen to punch a number on the telephone. She crossed her legs, flashing expensive shoe leather and toned thighs. The other woman removed papers from her briefcase and leaned toward the first woman as soon as she'd completed her call.

As they discussed the papers, they effectively blocked Rose's only escape route. Rose pretended to read a back issue of an advertising trade magazine and surreptitiously dragged her hobo bag under her skirt.

A courier pushed his way into the reception area and handed a document package to the receptionist. She signed for it, made a note, then left her desk and hurried down the hall.

Now. Now was Rose's chance to escape. She heard a door open and the sound of male voices. Jumping to her feet, she took a step, forgetting about her purse. The strap dragged on her foot and Rose lost precious seconds untangling it.

The rumbling voices grew louder, punctuated by bursts of male laughter. "We still on for racquetball Thursday, Duncan?"

Involuntarily, Rose looked up, searching for the man who was Duncan.

Four men stood beside the doors. Three wore suits and one was in his shirtsleeves, which glowed whitely against the charcoal and navy of the suits. "I have a standing four-thirty court time," he was saying as he held out his hand for one of the men to shake.

Mr. Shirtsleeves was Duncan Burke.

"Oh, my," Rose whispered.

Everyone else in the vicinity faded into shadow as the glow of Duncan's shirt increased to the intensity of a spotlight. Rose could swear she heard a chorus singing his name in four-part harmony. Duncan Burke. *Duncan Burke*. DUNCAN BURKE!

As he shook each man's hand, he smiled, and she had to shade her eyes from the blinding whiteness.

It was too much. The lantern jaw, the cleft in his chin, the black hair and deep blue eyes. The way one small wave parted from the rest and caressed his forehead. His height, his shoulders, his stomach, or rather lack of one. The rumbling bass of his voice.

She, Rose Franklin, had found the perfect man. There he was. The one. *The* one man worthy of a certain size eight, pearl-encrusted bridal gown with cathedral-length train, slightly worn.

In fact, Rose wasn't certain if the dress was worthy of him.

She forgot where she was and why. She only knew she had to step into the circle of light with him so they could live happily ever after, be fruitful and multiply.

Duncan walked the men to the elevators, with Rose unabashedly following his every move. Then he pivoted on his heel and came straight for her.

Of course. He must sense it, too. They were meant to be. Rose sighed at the wonder of it all and prepared to be swept off her feet.

Duncan pulled open the glass door and the very air in the room seemed charged with his presence. "Trisha, Mary Lynn, sorry to keep you waiting."

"We were early." The women stood.

Rose trembled.

"I think we've made a decision," the one with the briefcase said as they moved past the chairs.

Duncan murmured something and sent a brief, quizzical glance toward Rose.

Rose's knees melted. That could be the only possible explanation for tripping over her lumpy purse again.

She dropped the planner as she tried to catch her balance. Just before she fell, she saw a flash of white and felt strong arms encircle her waist. Duncan's arms.

She looked up and found herself inches away from the handsomest human being she'd ever seen or imagined. His ink blue eyes were warm with concern, his lips—perfectly shaped lips—were parted. His head tilted. Rose closed her eyes.

"Are you all right?" Duncan steadied her, then removed his arms from her waist.

Rose, who had been leaning heavily on him, nearly fell again. "Yes," she breathed, her eyes wide open now.

Duncan bent and picked something up from the floor. "Here you go," he said, handing her the planner. *His* planner. "Hang on to this. I recently lost one like it and can hardly function."

Rose could only gape.

Duncan smiled one last time at her, then nodded to the women and left.

Don't go, she wanted to call after him. *Don't you want to know my name?*

She stared after Duncan as he led the two women down the hallway.

He didn't look back.

Rose stood as if in a trance until the receptionist returned.

"Did you miss Mr. Burke?" The woman glanced down the hall where he'd gone, then back to Rose.

"I..." Rose's voice trailed off as she realized she was still holding the planner clutched to her chest. She'd forgotten all about it. Now she hugged it tighter, unwilling to relinquish it just yet. Unwilling to hand it over until she could have Duncan Burke's undivided attention. Until she was worthy of his undivided attention.

"Let me page him for you." The receptionist reached for the telephone.

"No!" Rose grabbed her purse and guiltily shoved the planner inside. "We spoke."

A beeping telephone claimed the receptionist's attention and Rose slipped out the doors.

She'd be back, she vowed. And the next time, she'd be so elegant and fascinating and charming that Duncan Burke wouldn't *want* to walk away from her.

CHAPTER TWO

STILL dazed when she arrived back at her shop, Rose, clutching the planner protectively to her breast, slipped through the back door and went directly to her tiny office beneath the stairs.

"Rose, that better be you!" Connie called.

"Yes, I'm back," Rose replied, amazed that her voice sounded entirely normal when her whole focus in life had completely changed. "I've got paperwork to take care of," she added, knowing how Connie loathed paperwork.

"Gotcha," Connie acknowledged and was blessedly silent.

Rose swept inventory sheets to one side and placed the planner square on her desk. A scrape arced across the coffee-colored leather and the rounded edges were worn to a café au lait color. Rose traced the scrape with one unadorned finger, then, propping her elbows on the desktop, she rested her chin in her hands and gazed at the zippered book that held the secrets to Duncan Burke's life.

It was a busy, active life. That she knew already. And he led it in a modern setting, surrounded by confident, vibrant, attractive people.

Duncan Burke charged through life while Rose Franklin dealt in life's leftovers.

19

She gazed at the bulging planner, remembering the quantity of papers inside. Duncan would be the sort of man who made things happen for himself. Rose had been waiting for life to happen *to* her.

But nothing ever happened, except this morning, when she found the planner and was led to Duncan Burke.

It was a sign. Before her, Rose had an opportunity. She could ignore it by leaving the planner with his receptionist and never see Duncan Burke again. Or, she could knock on the door of Duncan's life and see if he'd let her in.

And she wanted in, oh, how she wanted in. Even without knowing anything more about him, she knew that he led the life of her dreams, the one she wished she led but didn't quite know how.

Picking up the planner, she held it against her cheek and sighed, then inhaled more deeply. Leather smell, of course, but more. Garlic. She smiled, imagining business lunches in Italian restaurants. A sweet, musky scent…the base notes of after-shave—or a woman's perfume. A surprising mint and—she wrinkled her nose—a distinct locker-room odor. Also cigarettes and something indefinable that Rose thought might be Duncan himself.

Fate had sent her his planner, Rose decided. She would be going against fate if she ignored it. Reading the personal minutiae of Duncan's life would be an invasion of his privacy. It would be wrong, but it was necessary if she wanted to learn. She would think of the planner as a guidebook to an unfamiliar world. Duncan's world.

Leaning out from her desk to check on Connie, Rose unzipped the personal agenda of Duncan Burke. She waited for guilt to wash over her. Surprisingly, there was none. Rose smiled. Just as she'd suspected, it was fate.

A stick of chewing gum tucked in front of business cards explained the mint smell, and without even thinking about it, Rose noted the brand and flavor on a legal pad. Photocopying the whole book would be more efficient, but inexplicably, Rose felt that would be cheating.

At first, she confined her reading to Duncan's weekly calendar. All his appointments since January, both personal and professional, were listed. Duncan had a disconcerting habit of using initials instead of a person's name, but Rose dutifully copied down a whole alphabet of people anyway.

After two hours of furtive scribbling, during which she was interrupted less frequently by customers than she might have liked, Rose had a fairly accurate picture of Duncan Burke's daily life.

An organized man who cherished routine, Duncan preferred Italian food and had two favorite restaurants. He exercised at the expensive Texan Health Club and had a standing racquetball court time. Rose knew where he shopped, who his mechanic was, his dentist, his doctor, the florist he used and where his parents lived. She knew where *he* lived.

In fact, the only intimate detail of his life Rose didn't know was Duncan's financial profile. She'd scrupulously avoided looking at the divider marked "Finances". She didn't need to know anything about Duncan's financial dealings to try to become a part of his life. Invading his privacy was necessary. Snooping was not.

Stretching her arms above her head, Rose massaged the kink in her neck and pushed the folding chair back from the desk. Now she had to find something to wear. Something worthy of her meeting with Duncan.

Entering the main part of her shop, Rose headed for a rack of dresses as the grandfather clock chimed the half hour. Three-thirty. She'd have to hurry if she wanted to catch Duncan before he left his office for the day.

"Whatcha looking for?" Connie asked, lifting her head from a sea of reference books.

"An outfit to wear to a meeting," Rose answered vaguely, not certain whether to enlist Connie's aid or not.

"What kind of meeting?"

"An important meeting."

"Suits," Connie pronounced.

Remembering the polished women who'd had the meeting with Duncan, Rose knew Connie was right. She turned toward the slim number of muted grays and navy blues squeezed next to the winter coats.

"Is it a luncheon meeting?"

The question stopped Rose. By the time she fought the traffic and returned to Duncan's office today, it would be late. He might be gone. But if she went tomorrow morning, maybe he'd ask her to lunch at one of the Italian restaurants he liked. "Mmm, maybe." The idea of lunch with Duncan was both thrilling and frightening.

"Man or woman?"

"What?" Rose had picked out a good-looking, if severely cut navy blue suit. It and several others had belonged to a trial lawyer who was now a new mother.

"Is your meeting with a man or a woman?"

Rose started to answer "man", then hesitated, thinking again of the intimidating receptionist. "Both."

Connie pointed to the rack of consignment suits sent there by some of Houston's top society women. "Then you want one of those suits."

"Those aren't rentals," Rose said automatically. "They're for sale."

"They've been worn. Once more won't make a difference." Connie slipped from her stool behind the counter and approached the rack of colorful suits. "What kind of meeting is this anyway?"

A meeting with destiny. Rose swallowed. "Oh, I've been thinking that we need to advertise—"

"No kidding."

"And Mrs. Donahue gave me the name of a friend of her new son-in-law. One of the groomsmen in the wedding. He's in advertising." Amazing how slippery truth could be.

"Then you want a power suit." Connie fingered a red wool crepe and pulled it from the rack.

Rose tried to imagine herself wearing it. She didn't feel a surge of power and confidence. "No," she said, hanging the suit back up. "It's too much."

"Women will be at this meeting, too, huh?" Connie reached for a plastic-covered suit. "This is the one you need," she said as she unzipped the bag.

"I can't wear that!" Rose stared from the pastel blue bouclé knit to her legs. "It's way too short—and it's so expensive!"

"Of course it's expensive—it's a Chanel!" Connie handled it reverently. "And these cute little interlocking Cs on the buttons will tell everyone so."

"But—"

"Try it on." Connie thrust the jacket at her.

Rose shook her head. "It belongs to Mrs. Larchwood."

"It's been hanging here for a year and a half. She won't let us mark it down any cheaper and nobody is going to pay nine hundred dollars for it no matter how much it cost when it was new." Connie pulled off Rose's vest and held out the jacket.

"I shouldn't." Even as she protested, Rose slipped her arms into it.

"I never understood why Mrs. Larchwood didn't want this suit anymore," Connie commented.

Pulling the edges together, Rose buttoned the jacket. The fit was snug, but she wouldn't be wearing a blouse under it. "Because this suit was on the cover of every major fashion magazine that spring. By the time Mrs. Larchwood started wearing the suit, everybody had already seen it and it looked old. Besides, Carolina Markham has the same suit in yellow. They showed up at some luncheon wearing them at the same time."

"Oops. Well, it's still a great suit. Try on the skirt," Connie urged her.

Rose stepped behind one of the dividing screens that served as a dressing room and slipped out of her denim skirt and into the short knit one. An awful lot of leg was showing. Doubtfully, she eyed herself in the antique mirror.

Connie stuck her head around the edge of the screen. "Fab!"

"Fat! I look fat?"

"No, I said *fab*. You look great."

"I don't know." Rose didn't think she looked as chic as the two women and the receptionist, designer suit or not.

Connie fingered the hem. "Feel the chain? That's to keep it hanging flat." She sighed.

Rose turned to one side. "Do you think the skirt's too tight?" After her denim and her loose, flowing or full skirts, Rose felt exposed.

"Absolutely not!" Connie assured her and tugged at the jacket. "You've got a great figure. You should show it off more."

Rose still wasn't convinced. "Something's not right."

"Because you aren't wearing any shoes." Connie moved to the accessory counter. "The whole outfit'll look great when we find the right shoes and purse. And earrings." She rummaged through the costume jewelry, settling on a pair of sedate gold button earrings. "We don't want to overdo."

But after they'd scrounged everything they could scrounge, Connie was forced to agree with Rose. Something was off.

"It's your hair," Connie said at last.

"What's wrong with my hair?" Self-consciously, Rose brushed the ends behind her shoulders, then gathered it behind her neck. "Maybe I should pull it back?"

"No, it needs some oomph. I'll call Mark." Connie reached for the telephone.

"No!" Rose shouted, then deliberately lowered her voice when she saw Connie's hurt expression. "I—it's too much trouble. I'll just wear something else." Connie's boyfriend, Mark Mulot, was an aspiring hairdresser with an apprenticeship right here in the Village. That was one reason Connie liked working at Rose's Attic. But Mark was rather avant-garde in his styling and was having difficulty building a regular clientele.

"Oh, Rose, please! I know Mark could work you in today!"

And Rose knew why. "I couldn't—" she frantically unbuttoned the jacket "—Connie, don't—"

But Connie had already dialed the number on the old-fashioned telephone and was excitedly speaking to her boyfriend.

Rose hung up the suit and gave herself a pep talk. No matter how much it hurt Connie's feelings, Rose wasn't going to sacrifice her hair to Mark's unorthodox vision.

Rose sat in the vinyl chair with a tie-dyed cape swirled around her shoulders. "Well, I was thinking just a trim..."

"She's wearing this." Connie, who had dragged both Rose and the suit over to Harmonic Visions Hair Salon, held up the powder blue suit. "Just look."

"No kiddin'?" Mark rubbed at a button. "Is it the real thing?"

At both Rose's and Connie's nods, Mark got a gleam in his eye.

"I was thinking just a trim," Rose repeated, her desperation audible.

"A pricey outfit like that deserves more than a trim." Mark combed through Rose's hair.

"She needs oomph," added Connie helpfully.

Horrified at what Mark's definition of "oomph" might be, Rose sought a compromise she could live with. "Maybe some subtle highlights... b-blond?"

Mark's eyes lit up.

Uh-oh. "Well, gold. A golden brown actually," Rose amended hastily as Mark began pulling bottles off the shelf. "And only a few streaks... just a shade or so lighter...more of a hint than an actual color change..."

"Oh, Rose!" Connie clasped her hands together. "You look just like a Dallas socialite."

"My hair is blond." Rose stared at herself in the shop mirror, still unable to believe the events that had transpired at the Harmonic Visions Hair Salon yesterday evening. She'd actually allowed Mark, who had come to the shop this morning to "comb her out", to streak her hair.

And streak he had. In fact, there were more streaks than unstreaks.

"You like it, don't you?" Standing behind her, he smiled eagerly.

"It's blond."

"You said blond."

"Only once. I said light brown a bunch of times after that."

"But look." Mark whisked away the cape. "The suit cries for blond."

Rose felt like crying, too. "I don't even look like myself," she murmured. Of course, it could be because she wasn't wearing her glasses. Glasses spoiled the look, everyone agreed.

Connie threw up her hands. "I thought you didn't *want* to look like yourself!"

In the mirror, Rose could see her assistant's gaze dart to Mark, who had gone all quiet. Well, Rose was the one who had started mentioning color and she *had* said blond. She turned her head, noting how the morning sunlight glinted off the golden strands. Her hair had never glinted when it was brown.

"I'm just not used to the color yet, I guess," she said and smiled at Mark, trying to reassure them both at the same time.

Mark relaxed and squirted her with more hair spray.

And that was something else. "It...doesn't move." Rose shook her head to illustrate.

"We don't want it to move," Mark pronounced. "It's structured, echoing the lines of the suit." He followed the curve of her hair with his hands. "We've evoked the *C*s. It's a very sophisticated look, like the suit."

Connie handed her the earrings and Rose clipped them on. She stood and stared at herself.

"Wow," Connie breathed.

With her hair and the stronger makeup Connie had insisted she apply, Rose looked sophisticated. Worldly. Even a bit glamorous. She looked like Duncan Burke's sort of woman. She tilted her chin up, ready to do battle with the receptionists of the world.

"Hey." Obviously pleased, Mark grinned. "Look what I did."

"*We* did," Connie amended. "Okay, Rose. Go get 'em."

"Wait!" Mark dug in his pockets. "Let me give you some of my business cards. You know, in case someone wants to know who did your hair."

Rose practiced various ways to approach Duncan on the drive to his office. She might be sophisticated on the outside, but she was still the same old Rose on the inside.

What if the receptionist recognized her?

Or what if Duncan wasn't there?

Rose gripped the steering wheel. He would be there. He had to be. The same fate that had sent her to him would see that he was there when she arrived.

Yes, they were fated to meet. And no snooty receptionist was going to stand between Rose Franklin and fate.

Rose swept off the elevator and into the Burke and Bernard reception area with a fixed but determined smile on her face.

The same receptionist sat behind the curved island. "May I help you?" she asked even before Rose was close enough to show off her suit buttons.

"Oh, I hope so!" Rose said breezily. "I don't have an appointment, but *please* tell me Duncan Burke is in."

The receptionist reached for the telephone. "Whom shall I say is asking for him?"

"Rose Franklin, but the name won't mean anything to him."

The receptionist hesitated, her gaze sweeping over Rose before fastening on the suit buttons.

"However, Stephanie Donahue and her mother are clients of mine," Rose added, hoping the receptionist wouldn't ask what sort of clients. "Duncan was in the wedding last weekend."

"And the nature of your business with Mr. Burke is...?"

"Personal." Rose met the woman's gaze and held it, determined not to look away first.

Victory came faster than she'd expected.

"One moment."

The young woman hurried down the hall instead of using the phone. No doubt she wanted to talk to Duncan in private about the mysterious—but sophisticated— woman in the reception area.

Rose let out her breath. She'd passed the first hurdle! At this point, she would've sat down, except her knees were quivering and she was afraid she wouldn't be able to rise gracefully when Duncan arrived.

When Duncan arrived. Rose closed her eyes to steady herself. Where should she stand? What should she be doing? She needed props like a cellular phone or a personal planner of her own.

The planner! Rose whisked it behind her because she didn't want Duncan to see it until she'd had a chance to gauge his reaction to her. So far, the receptionist hadn't recognized her as the clumsy, denim-clad, mousy-haired female from yesterday, but Duncan had seen her—*truly* seen her. He'd gazed into her eyes. Feelings had passed between them. Rose had felt emotions so powerful that Duncan *must* have felt them, too.

But what if he *hadn't* felt those feelings? What would she say if he took one look at her and said, "*You* again?"

Nonsense. Even her own mother wouldn't recognize her.

"Ms. Franklin?"

Rose's eyes popped open.

Duncan Burke strode toward her, followed by his curious receptionist. He'd taken the time to put on his suit jacket, and the dark fabric contrasted with his white shirt.

Office sounds faded away as sweet heavenly trumpets heralded his arrival. Darkness edged her peripheral vision while all the light in the room focused in a hazy glow on Duncan. Nothing existed except Duncan. Time slowed as once more Rose was enchanted by his magic.

He was the one. Really and truly. And he must know it, too. Even from this distance, Rose could see his incredibly blue eyes gazing into her nearsighted ones. The two of them were being drawn together by forces greater than either of them.

And then he was standing there, so close she could see the shadows made by the tangle of his lashes. "I'm Duncan Burke," he said, as if she wouldn't know. He smiled, this time for her alone, held out his hand and took hers in a firm, warm grasp.

Rose could feel the energy flow from him and she didn't want to let go. She never wanted to let go. "I'm Rose Franklin," she breathed, reluctantly releasing his hand when she felt his grip relax. Once she was no longer touching him, Rose could think again. "I'm sorry we didn't get a chance to meet at the Donahue wedding," she said just as she'd practiced.

"So am I." His voice rumbled toward her in waves that lapped at the shore of her soul.

Duncan accompanied the bit of gallantry with a smile so charming, Rose nearly lost her place in her speech.

"Somehow, which I'm sure is a *very* interesting story, this—" Rose held up the planner "—became mixed in with the bridesmaids' clothing."

"My planner!" He took it from her with a look of delighted surprise. "You angel!"

He'd called her an angel. Rose tried to remember to breathe.

"I haven't been able to function for days." He unzipped it. "Everything's still in here." With an exaggerated sigh, he wiped his brow. "Lois, drop everything and photocopy every piece of paper in here for me, will you? I never want to go through this hassle again."

Lois, the receptionist, looked from Duncan to Rose before taking the planner. Rose smiled at her. Lois didn't smile back.

Duncan touched Rose's elbow. "Ms. Franklin...Rose is it?"

Rose nodded. She loved the way he said her name.

Duncan's brows drew together. "I feel I've seen you before. Are you certain we didn't meet at the wedding?"

"*Very* certain," Rose said firmly.

The crease between his black brows eased. "Anyway, I can't begin to tell you how relieved I am to get that organizer back. How did you find it?"

"Oh, I can't take the credit. Mrs. Donahue found it when she was going through the bridesmaids' paraphernalia. She's still busy with out-of-town company, and since I had errands on this side of town, I offered to run it by." Rose was determined to tell the truth as much as possible. Inevitably, there would be times when some creative truth stretching would be in order, but this wasn't one of those times.

"You a friend of Stephanie's?" Duncan asked.

Now *this* might call for some stretching. "Her mother and I have worked together." Rose was trying to decide how much more detail she could supply when Duncan jumped to an acceptable conclusion.

"Oh, yeah, she's always doing those charity things." Duncan shook his head. "You know... I can't believe I missed you at the wedding." He studied her. "Although you do look familiar."

"You were busy," Rose inserted hastily. She didn't want him remembering exactly *why* she looked familiar. "The wedding was lovely, wasn't it? Did you know the bride wore a vintage dress?"

"Was it?" He shrugged. "All wedding dresses look alike to me."

She'd forgive him for that. He hadn't noticed the dress because he wasn't meant to yet. Rose hadn't been wearing it. When she wore it for him, *then* he'd notice it.

"Listen—" he checked his watch and then shoved his hands into his pockets "—are you free for lunch today? You've really saved my hide and I'd like to properly thank you."

"Lunch would be wonderful," Rose said, hardly daring to believe this was really happening. Yes, she'd plotted it all, but to have her scheme actually work was thrilling. "Besides, I still want to hear how *your* organizer got mixed in with the bridesmaids' clothing." Rose, who had planned to laugh in a flirty, sophisticated way, managed one squeak and gave up.

"Nothing scandalous, I'm afraid. I was using the telephone outside the dressing area and must have left the planner on the table there. Obviously, it was scooped up with all the other wedding debris.'' He chuckled and reached over the receptionist's island to scribble on a self-stick notepad. ''So what sort of meal are you in the mood for?''

''Italian,'' Rose replied, ready to suggest one of his favorite restaurants if he didn't.

''You like Italian food?'' Duncan grinned as he finished writing, tore off the note and stuck it to the switchboard. ''I know this great little place...''

She'd made it this far. Her plan was working. She'd wangled a lunch invitation from him. She was going to talk with him. She was going to fascinate him.

She was going to throw up.

CHAPTER THREE

ROSE had discovered a great truth. There was no greater stress than that caused by wearing a borrowed powder blue Chanel suit while attempting to eat fettuccine with marinara sauce.

What had possessed her? The oily Caesar salad with sun-dried tomatoes had been ordeal enough. She should've stopped there, but Duncan had ordered a salad and main dish, and Rose didn't want to sit there without anything to do while he ate.

The oval plate was piled so high with the treacherous pasta strands that Rose couldn't even push around a few and pretend to eat. The whole glob would probably slide right off the plate and onto the pristine white tablecloth. Glancing at the other diners, she saw that nobody else seemed concerned about eating. No, everybody was chatting and laughing and being sophisticated.

She should have ordered lasagna, which could be cut with a fork into small, neat cubes. White cheese vegetarian lasagna would have been ideal, but Rose was trying to be sophisticated and fettuccine sounded so much more sophisticated than lasagna.

Duncan had ordered lasagna.

Rose sighed and separated one red sauce-laden noodle from the rest and gently rolled it over her fork. An inch-long end dangled. Why was fettuccine made in that length? Just a bit shorter or a bit longer and it would be so much more convenient to eat. Didn't fettuccine makers eat their own product? If they did, Rose was certain all their ties were splattered with various sauces.

"Is something wrong?" Duncan paused, a neat forkful of lasagna poised above his plate.

Yes, I'm one drip away from spending nine hundred dollars for this suit. "No, everything's lovely." She looked at her mound of pasta and tried to think of something to say. "The portions are very generous." Oh, no. Now he'd think she was criticizing his choice of a restaurant.

A corner of his mouth tilted upward. "I won't tell your mother if you don't clean your plate."

Which was a good thing, since her frugal mother would have been horrified at the waste. In fact, Rose's small-town parents couldn't begin to understand what strange forces had compelled Rose to don the priciest item in her inventory, dye her hair and worry about charming the man sitting across from her in a chic little Italian restaurant. Rose wasn't sure she understood those forces, either.

Duncan was watching her, one black brow arched quizzically. Rose knew she was going to have to ferry the fettuccine from her plate to her mouth, gracefully and driplessly—and soon.

Concentrating, she lifted her fork and a second later closed her mouth around the pasta in relief. She smiled at Duncan, who was still watching her. He smiled back and continued to eat.

Only three million more strands to go.

It was time for wit and charm. They'd already pretty much exhausted the topic of the wedding that Rose hadn't attended, and Rose knew they had no mutual friends.

What did witty, sophisticated people talk about anyway?

"What do you think about the Astros' chances of making it to the World Series this year?" Duncan asked.

Witty, sophisticated people must discuss baseball, Rose deduced. She knew very little about baseball or the various teams. "It's hard to say," she hedged, trying to remember everything she'd read about Houston's baseball team. "The Astros never seem to perform the way you think they should."

"Isn't that the truth," Duncan said with a heartfelt sigh.

Her comment must not have been too out of line. Rose felt bolder. "Are you a fan? Do you have season tickets?"

"The agency has a skybox at the Dome," Duncan said. "I go to as many of the games as I can, but since the whole purpose of having a box is to entertain clients, I don't get to relax and just watch the field very often."

"I've never been to a game in the Astrodome," Rose said wistfully, then wanted to bite back the words. He'd think she was hinting for an invitation! Or worse, wonder what kind of Houstonian had never been to the Astrodome. "I'm not much of a sports fan."

"No?" He smiled briefly and continued to eat.

And why had she said *that*? She'd killed sports as a conversational topic—not that she could have added much—and by implication, criticized Duncan for liking sports. "What I meant," she added, trying to salvage the conversation, "was that a true sports fan supports her team whether they're winning or losing. I'm afraid I only like to watch when they're winning."

Duncan chuckled. "And since the Astros are so seldom winning...no, that's not true. They come close, but manage to lose the big games. They get a lead and start playing too safe." Leaning on his forearms, Duncan looked at her intently. "It's late in the game when you're ahead that you've got to play the hardest, because that's when the other team's going to throw everything they've got at you. At that point, the game is theirs to win and yours to lose."

This all sounded very profound to Rose. "Are you speaking from experience?" she asked.

Duncan raised a shoulder as he resumed eating. "I batted a ball or two when I was in school."

Which probably meant he was some huge college star she should have heard of. Rose miserably twirled her fettuccine, almost not caring whether she splattered sauce on the suit or not.

"Coach used to tell us, 'Winners never quit and quitters never win'. I've found those to be pretty good words to live by." He glanced up at her. "What words do you live by, Rose?"

Some day my prince will come. It just popped into her head, but she couldn't very well tell Duncan that, no matter how pathetically true it was. "Do a good turn daily?"

He gave a crack of laughter. "Isn't that a Scout motto?"

"It could be. I was a Girl Scout."

"Well, returning my organizer was your good turn for today and I thank you very much."

"You're welcome." Rose couldn't think of anything else to say. This business of being witty and charming was hard work—work for which she was ill-prepared. There was nothing about her life that would remotely interest Duncan Burke. Her life didn't even interest *her*. Perhaps she should go back to her original plan of getting free advertising advice.

The silence between them was about to become uncomfortable. Rose hastily took a bite of her lunch, acutely conscious that she wasn't holding up her end of the conversation. She had to think of some thought-provoking topic.

Duncan beat her to it once again. "So, how do you spend your days, Rose?"

More than a yes-or-no response was called for here and the question, or a variation of it, was one Rose had anticipated. She picked up her water glass. "I own a clothing boutique in the Village." Boutique sounded much better than resale and consignment shop.

"I know that area." A spark of interest lit his eyes. "Rice Village, right?"

Rose nodded.

"I teach a marketing course at Rice University on Thursday nights."

That explained the blocked-off time in his planner on Thursdays. Rose immediately resolved to sign up for classes in continuing education at Rice. "You must stay very busy." As if she didn't know.

"What do you mean?"

"Well, I know your advertising agency is terribly successful. I recognized several of the ads for products you have displayed on the walls."

"I'd say we've been lucky, but Robert and I have worked too hard to give luck all the credit." Duncan gave her a frank smile, then murmured his assent to the waiter, who'd offered to pour more iced tea.

Rose was much struck by Duncan's words. She, too, had worked hard, and how many times had she attributed her modest success to luck? "Did you and your partner start the agency yourselves?"

"Yes. And we did it the hard way, by making cold calls and doing whole campaigns on spec. We lived on money we borrowed from every friend and relative whose arms we could twist."

As Duncan talked about the years when he and Robert Bernard were starting out, Rose's admiration for him grew. He had believed in himself and had taken chances. That's why he was living the good life now. And Duncan had never stopped working. Thinking back to Mrs. Donahue's description of his activities at the wedding, Rose thought maybe he was working *too* much.

Winners never quit and quitters never win.

In both her professional and personal lives, Rose had been coasting for the past several years. *Some day my prince will come.* She'd failed to invest any more of herself into Rose's Attic because deep down, she expected a man to sweep her off her feet. But how was a man going to find her, buried as she was in a women's secondhand clothing shop?

Duncan had found her, or rather, she'd found Duncan. But Rose would have to work to keep his interest. She thought hard. In conversation, Duncan asked the sort of questions that probed beneath the surface. If she didn't want him to find her shallow, she'd better start filling her pool.

He'd been discussing various campaigns and how they'd come about. Maybe she could comment on some aspect of his work. "I've discovered there's a certain psychology involved in selling to people," Rose ventured, daring to draw parallels between her modest experience and his. "Many times, women are buying more than just the outfit. They're buying the idea of the kind of person they'll be when they wear it."

"Exactly!" For the first time during their lunch, Duncan seemed truly caught up in a topic Rose had introduced. She savored the warm satisfaction she felt. "First you have to sell people on the idea of fun, or happiness, or beauty, or whatever, then they'll want the product. Now take our ads for Vanguard bicycle helmets."

Duncan was lit by a fire within. His expression was intent, his voice compelling and self-assured. While he spoke, he gestured with his hands, punctuating the key points. Rose imagined him pitching ad campaigns. No wonder he'd made a success of Burke and Bernard.

"Kids don't care about safety, but their parents do," Duncan was saying. "If the kids think they look stupid wearing a helmet, they're not going to, and frankly—" he spread his hands in dismissal "—unless a parent is prepared to follow them all over the neighborhood, they can't make their children keep those helmets on." Here, Duncan leaned forward. Rose noticed he did this when he was about to impart something important. "So, Rob and I geared our campaign to the kids and stressed how cool they could look wearing a helmet."

"Hey, not just kids, either," Rose said. "I have a Vanguard helmet, too."

"Do you?" He seemed pleased. "What made you buy one?"

"The wild colors," she confessed, embarrassed that the design had been more important to her than the safety features.

"Vanguard helmets didn't have all the colors until I talked them into it." Duncan grinned and Rose grinned back. "Not that the designs are the only thing going for those helmets. They *are* a good product. Otherwise, we wouldn't have taken them on. I won't try to sell something I don't believe in."

"That's very admirable," Rose commented, though she would have expected nothing less of Duncan.

"It's also good business." He paused to take a drink of his tea. "I think our honesty comes through in our advertisements and makes them more effective."

After that, the conversation flowed more easily, though Rose never did feel comfortable battling her fettuccine and regretfully allowed the waiter to remove most of it.

"Would you care for coffee?" Duncan asked.

Rose would have liked to prolong lunch, but she'd seen Duncan discreetly checking his watch. He was a busy man. Of course he'd have obligations this afternoon. She shouldn't keep him from the office any longer, though she'd naively hoped he'd be so fascinated by her he'd lose track of time. Now that she knew it would take someone knowledgeable and dynamic to fascinate Duncan, she'd work on becoming that person. "No, thank you," she said, declining the coffee. "We should probably be getting back."

She knew she'd made the right decision when, without further comment, Duncan quickly dealt with the check by signing his name to it and ushered her toward the valet parking. In moments, the attendant arrived in Duncan's BMW.

He must have an account at the restaurant. Rose had never seen anyone pay by just signing his name. And Duncan hadn't spoken to anyone on their way to the exit, yet his car was brought around.

This was how important people dealt with life, Rose thought as she slid across the leather seat. Other people took care of the small details for them.

"Where do you travel on buying trips for your boutique?" Duncan asked as he merged his car into the traffic.

"Oh, here and there." Rose felt a pang. She longed to travel and see the world, but she never had. And Duncan obviously assumed her shop was much more exclusive than it was. "I think buying trips sound more glamorous than they actually are," she added, hoping he wouldn't pursue the topic.

She wasn't ashamed of Rose's Attic, but for now, she'd rather Duncan not know exactly how modest her circumstances were.

"Advertising is another field that appears more glamorous than it really is," Duncan commented. "But then, advertising is built on appearances, isn't it?"

"I suppose so," Rose agreed, wondering if Duncan thought that was a bad thing. She couldn't decide.

They were right in the middle of a conversation about product placement in movies when Rose suddenly thought about her car. She drove an eight-year-old, bottom-of-the-line car with its finish ruined by years of parking under the dripping cottonwood trees.

If Duncan saw her junky car, her whole image would be spoiled. What could she do?

They were at the stoplight at the corner of Post Oak and Westheimer, right next to the Galleria. Duncan's office building was within sight. Rose's heart started beating faster. Duncan would want to drive her to her car since there was no reason for her to return to his office.

Sure enough... "What floor did you park on?"

Rose desperately tried to think of a reason for Duncan to let her off somewhere else. The whole area was littered with exclusive shops, but in her panic, she couldn't think of the name of a single one. "Third."

Actually, Rose couldn't even remember if that *was* her floor. Now he'd think she was scatterbrained.

They approached the garage and Duncan waved to the attendant, who raised the wooden bar and let him through the contract parking side.

They spiraled upward. Rose began to sweat. The instant they exited onto the third floor, Rose spotted her car. On either side of it was a glittering import.

"Which one?" Duncan asked as they crawled by the cars.

Rose's tongue stuck to the roof of her mouth.

Duncan passed by the faded red car.

"Th-there." Rose pointed a trembling finger toward a charcoal gray Mercedes. "You can let me off here."

Smiling as widely as she could, she opened her door. "I know you're busy, so I'll just hop out. Thanks for lunch. I enjoyed meeting you."

Duncan stretched his arm across the seat back. "Wait, I—"

Rose leaped from the car and hurried around to the driver's side. Ducking to look in the window, she burbled, "Thanks again. Don't let me keep you!" Stepping back, she waved frantically.

"At least let me make sure you're safely in the car," Duncan protested.

"Don't be silly!" She laughed, sounding silly herself.

He looked as though he'd challenge her on this, so Rose actually approached the Mercedes and dug in her purse, looking up and waving again when she didn't hear the car drive away. *Please go away!* Giving him a mock frown, she pointed sternly down the parking aisle, then waggled her fingers.

He didn't move.

Finally, Rose called to him, "I'm a wretched driver and I'm not about to humiliate myself by demonstrating how easily I get stuck in parking garages. Go!" She shooed him away with her hands.

His face eased as he broke into an understanding chuckle. "I should have known!" With a wave, he drove off and turned the corner to the next level.

The inner lining of the expensive suit was drenched and Rose's heart was just beginning to slow. That was close, but she'd escaped. Drawing a deep breath, she let it out in a sigh and trudged downhill to her car. All in all, she'd count lunch as a success. Duncan couldn't have been bored the entire time. Rose had managed to introduce one or two topics he'd found interesting.

Unlocking her car, she decided she'd have to study his interests more. Maybe check a book or two out from the library. And hadn't she seen a notice that the summer session at Rice was just getting under way? Maybe there was still time to sign up for a course—a course that met on Thursday nights. It would have to be something other than marketing, though. If she showed up in Duncan's class after their discussion, it would look like she was chasing him.

Rose sat on the cracked vinyl seat and slammed the door shut, the familiar rattle annoying her after the quiet luxury of Duncan's car. She cranked the motor, which teased her for several seconds before catching, then stomped on the accelerator. Her car coughed blue smoke, but stayed running.

Backing out of the parking place, Rose headed for the exit, reaching it just in time to see Duncan striding inside the office building.

Sighing, Rose stared after him. She could hardly wait to see him again. She wondered when he'd call her. She ought to warn Connie in case he...

A sick feeling spread through Rose's middle. She hadn't given Duncan Burke her phone number and he hadn't asked for it, either. He could still call her at the shop—if he'd known its name. But she hadn't ever told him the name, had she? All Duncan Burke knew about her was that she was a friend of the Donahues and she owned a boutique in the Village.

What if he called Mrs. Donahue and asked about Rose Franklin? He'd find out she hadn't been invited to the wedding. He'd realize she was a nobody. A fake. A fraud.

Not necessarily. As one part of her squirmed with dread, a more rational part pointed out that if Duncan just asked Mrs. Donahue if she had Rose's phone number, it was possible that Rose's precise connection with the Donahue family wouldn't come up.

Unfortunately, this cool, rational part of Rose also knew Duncan wasn't going to call her or Mrs. Donahue. If he'd wanted to see her again, he would have asked for her phone number. But he hadn't.

The old Rose would have moped about her shop for days, wishing for what might have been. The new Rose parked her car and didn't even change out of the borrowed suit before going directly to her office and studying the notes from Duncan's organizer.

She'd just have to plan to run into him somewhere. And when she did, she'd be more prepared to converse with him. Obviously, Duncan didn't yet realize they were meant to be. He needed more time and Rose would have to see that he got it.

"Connie, I'm back," she belatedly warned her assistant.

"How'd your meeting go?" Connie appeared in the doorway of Rose's office. "Did you knock 'em dead?"

"The suit was perfect," Rose told her.

"And your hair and makeup?"

Rose remembered how the receptionist had treated her this time and nodded. "The hair worked." She patted it and heard a crackle. "Maybe next time, we could go for something softer."

Connie's eyebrows rose. "Is there going to be a next time?"

Rose stared at the papers on her desk. "You bet there's going to be a next time." She just had to figure out where and when.

Where looked like it might be the Texan Health Club. According to his planner, Duncan had a membership there. Lots of people worked out at health clubs, right? So if Rose just happened to be at the Texan Health Club at the same time Duncan was arriving for his standing racquetball game... or better yet, *leaving* from his standing racquetball game, what could be more natural? Yes, now that she thought about it, running into him after his game would be best. Exercise cleared the mind. He'd be tired, but alert. She'd invite him to join her for a drink at the juice bar. The veil would be lifted from his eyes and he'd see that she was perfect for him. Yes, right then, Duncan would realize that Rose was the woman for him. He might even suggest dinner that night. A perfectly romantic dinner where he'd declare his everlasting love. She'd smile knowingly and agree to marry him. Rose sighed at the wonder of it all.

So, Wednesday morning found her at the Texan Health Club. It occupied the entire top floor of the Post Oak Hotel, a modern structure nestled in exclusive wooded acreage near Duncan's office. The hotel was part of a complex widely used as an urban retreat and conference center. A few hundred yards away was a section of the busiest freeway in Texas, but the leafy arms of the oak trees acted as both a sound barrier and a visual shield. No wonder Duncan was a member here. Such a vibrant man needed a place to relax and recharge. Rose herself felt calmer just driving up the narrow roadway.

But as Rose soon learned, such verdant surroundings came with a price. A steep price.

"Five thousand dollars?" She gaped at the white-uniformed young man who had quoted her the price of the health-club membership.

"That's only a one-time initiation fee," Jon, according to his name tag, explained, obviously thinking he was reassuring her. "Yearly membership is thirty-five hundred."

Rose swallowed. "Do you offer memberships for less than a year? Say a month just to try the facilities?"

"No." His smile narrowed. "Though we offer members' guests a one-day pass."

In other words, Rose would have to be vouched for by someone. Maybe Duncan would vouch for her. In fact, that would be an ideal excuse for her to contact him. No. For her plan to work, she'd have to already *be* a member.

"But I must be honest with you," Jon said with pseudo regret. He'd already dismissed her, Rose could tell. "We currently have a waiting list."

Enough people could afford to sweat here that there was a *waiting* list?

As Rose stood there, a couple approached the manager's desk and handed the young man a room key. He went to the computer, tapped on the keyboard, then nodded. "Shall I add the fee to your room?" When they nodded, Jon punched in a number and smiled. "Enjoy your workout."

"Hotel guests have health-club privileges?" Rose asked, an idea forming.

"Yes . . . are you a guest of the hotel?"

Just then, the desk phone rang and Jon turned to answer it.

Not yet, Rose thought.

She walked to the door of the club and looked in to check what people were wearing. Cute spandex exercise outfits. She sighed. Her shop didn't carry exercise clothing, so she'd have to buy shoes and a new outfit.

Which she'd do right after she made a room reservation at the Post Oak Hotel for tomorrow night.

CHAPTER FOUR

ON THURSDAY, Rose engineered her arrival at the Texan Health Club so she would already be using the machines by the time Duncan arrived. After much thought, she'd decided it would be better to run into Duncan after he finished his game. He'd be thirsty then, and her offer of a drink would seem natural. The problem was that Rose didn't know how long a game of racquetball took. She didn't know anything about racquetball.

As a matter of fact, she didn't know anything about the intimidating pieces of fitness equipment, either. But she sure looked good.

Rose closed her mind to the exorbitant sum she'd spent on various small, stretchy pieces of fabric. In pink. Rose didn't consider herself a pink sort of person, but pink looked different on her now. It must be her blond, or mostly blond hair.

She'd even bought a bottle holder and a bottle of Evian water, though she had every intention of refilling the bottle with ordinary tap water rather than paying for more. She had to cut costs somewhere.

Costs. She'd actually rented a room for the night just so she could use the health club. Rose shuddered and plopped her water bottle and towel by the stationary bicycle at the end of the row. *Don't think about it*, she instructed herself. Don't think about the outrageous cost of staying a single night in this place. Don't think about Connie being left in charge of Rose's Attic.

But of course, she did. Constantly. Even telling herself she was investing in her future didn't help.

Rose studied the bicycle. Controls for who-knew-what were between the handlebars. A lighted panel blinked Enter Weight, which Rose had no intention of doing. Calories Burned This Session flashed right under that. Never mind.

Gingerly, Rose got on the bicycle and started pedaling. The pedals moved as though she were pedaling up mountains. One of the controls must be for resistance.

After experimenting with the control panel, which looked as if it should be on the console of an aircraft rather than a bicycle, Rose found the pedals moved more easily and she settled in. The bike next to her was vacant, but the others were occupied. A man stared out into space as he pumped furiously. A couple of women read books.

Rose watched the people on the exercise machines so she could figure out how they worked. She knew the club personnel would be able to instruct her, but Rose didn't want to draw attention to herself by asking. She wanted to slip into this world quietly and easily, as though she belonged. Because, she vowed, someday she *would* belong.

At four twenty-five, Rose eyed the entrance to the men's locker room. She wasn't certain where the racquetball courts were located, but Duncan would surely change clothes before playing.

Four-thirty found Rose at a machine apparently used to torture the pectoral muscles. She was struggling to bring her forearms together in front of her face when Duncan and another man emerged from the locker room and ambled across the exercise area.

Immediately, Rose crashed her arms together and ducked her head. All would be spoiled if he saw her now.

Duncan wore navy shorts that exposed muscled thighs and a loose tank top revealing well-defined arms, shoulders and a broad chest. Slowly, Rose separated her arms so she could watch his progress. Moving with the solid grace of an athlete, he stopped once and hit the heel of his shoe with the baby tennis racquet he carried, then responded with a laugh to something his companion said.

Before now, Duncan Burke had been an ideal—the prince of her dreams. When Rose daydreamed about him, she'd always focused on his face, with the strong jaw and the flashing white teeth, the piercing blue eyes and well-shaped nose. Everything else was a pleasant, though hazy, blur. Duncan's face had floated about in her fantasies and she'd never given his body much thought.

That was about to change. Rose Franklin had just received a jolt of reality. Duncan Burke was a hunk.

She forgot what she was doing and the machine snapped her arms apart. Rose couldn't bring them together again. Duncan was a hunk and she was an out-of-shape blob.

"Would you like me to adjust the weight for you?" A fellow exerciser paused on his way to another machine.

Rose blinked up at him. His shoulders were so developed that he had no neck. "Uh, no. I think that'll do it for me today.'' And tomorrow and the day after, as well.

"You should take it a little easier next time. You can't make up for a lifetime of being out of shape in one afternoon.'' With that cheery observation, the man nodded and walked on.

A lifetime of being out of shape? Rose hadn't thought she was so out of shape, though perhaps she *was* depending too much on the girdlelike qualities of spandex.

As her quivering arms slithered to her sides, Duncan and the other man opened a door in the far wall and disappeared inside. The courts must be back there.

Although she wanted to leap up and run after him, Rose worked her way around the room, machine by machine, twisting, lifting and pulling, so no one would suspect that she was following Duncan. By the time she neared the machines closest to the door, she could barely walk. How was she supposed to open the door? She'd pulled her last pull.

Managing somehow, Rose found herself in a hallway that was bounded on either side by two Plexiglas-walled rooms. A door was at the opposite end, but Rose didn't bother exploring once she'd located Duncan and his partner.

They were in the middle of a fast-moving game, both men concentrating. Both men sweating.

Rose's mouth felt dry. Sweat had never looked so attractive. The corded muscles of Duncan's arms glistened. His hair curled damply over his forehead and he grimaced as he reached for and returned a shot.

Though sound was muffled by the glass, Rose could hear the thunk of balls bouncing and being hit, the squeak of rubber-soled shoes on the wooden floor and the occasional shouts and groans from the men. The other courts were also occupied, but Rose only watched Duncan and his partner.

She hardly spared the other man a glance. He was blondish and pale. Sweat only made him look damp, and not an attractive damp. Duncan mesmerized her. As he returned shot after shot, Rose watched the play of muscles across his back. This was a man in peak condition. Sports were clearly one of his interests, and if Rose wanted to be an interest, too, it was apparent that she would have to take up some sort of athletic activity. She should be working out with weights, too. Bicycling around the Village wasn't enough to keep her in shape, she'd discovered. She'd be sore tomorrow.

Duncan shouted and ran for a ball that bounced off the ceiling. His momentum propelled him to the window where Rose was watching. She scrambled backward involuntarily as Duncan crashed into the window, pushed off and positioned himself for the next shot. When she touched the fogged area on the Plexiglas, Rose could feel the lingering heat of his body.

He obviously hadn't seen her and Rose was glad. She'd planned for a "chance" meeting today, though she wasn't leaving anything up to mere luck.

She wished she had a close friend she could ask for advice. Working long hours by herself in the shop didn't leave her much time for socializing, and many of the women she'd known were now married and involved with their own families. Connie was probably the closest to a friend that Rose had right now, but Connie was a student and her employee. Rose didn't want to muddy that relationship by asking her for advice on men, though Connie had already guessed that a man was behind Rose's sudden interest in her appearance.

Duncan missed a shot, grimaced and looked skyward, but it was apparent from the grin he flashed at his partner that he wasn't angry. "Good shot!" Rose heard through the glass.

A good sportsman. Hardworking. A man's man. Handsome. Successful. Respected. Moderately wealthy, judging by what it cost to belong to the gym here. Rose sighed. Who wouldn't fall in love with such a man?

Rose wasn't immune, though she realized that knowing all about Duncan was not the same as knowing Duncan. And *that* was what she intended to rectify this afternoon.

With a last look at him, Rose returned to the main workout room and tried to sweat.

She had to settle for a glow, which might be preferable after all. Mark had carefully done her hair in what he called a "tousled exercise do" by gathering it into a loose ponytail on top of her head. Strategically placed tendrils spiraled at the sides and the back. Rose was considering pulling out a couple more to make it seem as if she'd been really working hard, when the back door opened and Duncan and the other man emerged.

Her heart started beating faster than it had the entire time she'd been exercising. Carefully, Rose began walking a wobbly path that would intercept Duncan's. *Please see me. Say something first. Act glad to have run into me. Offer me a drink so I don't have to make the first move.*

Chatting with his partner, Duncan swiped at his face and neck with a towel.

Fate may want her with Duncan, but fate wasn't making it easy. Rose was going to have to make the first move after all.

"Duncan?" Rose had practiced saying his name with just the right amount of pleased surprise.

He looked up, his face blank.

"Well, hello!" Rose smiled. She'd practiced that, too.

Without an answering smile, Duncan blinked, and in the next fraction of a second, Rose felt her heart freeze. *He doesn't remember who I am. He doesn't even recognize me. I've made no impression on him at all.*

Rose had anticipated everything but this. How could he have forgotten her? They'd had lunch together just two days ago!

She wanted to slink away. She wanted to crawl into a hole. She wanted to throw her towel over her head and hide.

Instead, she patted her stomach and gave him a clue. "I'm still working off that wonderful lunch we had the other day."

Recognition dawned. "Robert!" Duncan turned to the pale man next to him. "This is the angel who found my organizer."

A forgotten angel. Not only hadn't Duncan recognized her at first, he'd obviously forgotten her name.

It was obvious to the man standing next to him, as well. "Hi, I'm Robert Bernard," Duncan's partner said, offering his hand.

"Rose Franklin," Rose said loudly and distinctly.

"Thank you for returning Duncan's precious planner." Robert slid him a sideways glance. "I was ready to buy him a one-way ticket on the next flight out of here."

"Now, Robert, I wasn't that bad." Duncan's chuckle was a bit forced.

"Yes, you were." Robert saluted him with two fingers and backed away. "I'm heading for the showers. Nice to meet you, Rose."

At least *he* remembered her name. "And *I* was headed for the juice bar," Rose inserted before Duncan could follow Robert. "Care to join me?" Without giving him time to think about it and possibly decline her invitation, Rose began walking.

He'd *better* follow her! She'd dyed her hair for him. She'd navigated treacherous fettuccine for him. She'd tortured her muscles for him. By the time she paid for her hotel room, she was going to have spent nearly three hundred dollars on this "chance" meeting with him. He'd not dare to refuse to join her for a drink.

He caught up with her. "I haven't seen you around here before," he commented, draping his towel around his neck.

And he probably wouldn't have noticed her even if she'd been coming here daily. Rose had recovered from her first flash of hurt and was angry. Furious, actually, and she had no intention of analyzing whether or not her fury was justified. Duncan had wiped her from his memory because he had no plans to see her again. "This is my first visit," Rose told him. "I'm staying at the hotel while I'm having some renovations done." Connie was redoing the shop's display window. That counted as renovations, didn't it?

One thing her anger accomplished was to make Rose a lot less in awe of Duncan. He was human after all. He wasn't perfect. Close, but not entirely perfect.

"Ah." He slid onto a swiveling forest green bar stool and nodded to the woman behind the counter. She grabbed a glass and began mixing ingredients in a blender. "I thought I was really losing it not to have noticed you." He grinned at Rose so charmingly that she instantly forgave him. "But then again, I've had a lot on my mind lately."

"Now that you have your planner back, things should ease up, shouldn't they?"

"That helped, but I've been wrestling with an account." He stared off into space. "After an unbroken string of home runs, Burke and Bernard is about to strike out."

Rose started to question him, but the woman behind the counter approached her. "What can I get for you?"

Rose hesitated. What did people order here? There wasn't a menu posted over the cash register or anything so crass—but convenient—as that.

"Lisa knows I always have the same thing," Duncan said.

Lisa gave him a look that would have melted Lycra.

"I'll have what he's having," Rose said firmly and plopped her guest user's card with her room number on the counter.

"You might regret that," Duncan murmured.

"Why? What are you having?"

"Pineapple juice, carrot juice and wheat grass."

Rose just stopped herself from lying and saying it sounded delicious. "Grass?" Sure enough, Lisa pulled on a drawer that turned out to be a pallet of growing grass. Marking a square, she began snipping and throwing the grass clippings into the blender.

Rose turned to Duncan in astonishment.

Duncan winced. "I was thinking of cutting that stuff out, but it's supposed to be good for you."

"It has been my experience," said Rose, "that things that are good for you taste horrible."

"You are a wise woman, Rose," Duncan said as Lisa set two vaguely orange drinks in front of them.

Rose tapped her card, so Lisa would realize she wanted the charges on her bill. From her perch on the stationary bicycle, Rose had observed a number of people ordering at the juice bar and not once had she seen money change hands. Whatever signals they gave were casual and subtle. Rose hoped hers worked.

Apparently it did. Within seconds, Lisa presented Rose with a piece of paper. Rose quickly scrawled her name just the way she'd seen Duncan write his in the restaurant. Only Rose forgot to look at the amount. But how expensive could carrots and grass be anyway? It didn't matter. Things were proceeding nicely. Rose was in control of the situation.

"Thank you." Duncan raised his glass in a silent toast and took a swallow.

Rose, feeling very cosmopolitan, picked hers up and swiveled toward him. She crossed her legs and took a sip.

And gasped. "This smells like a compost heap!" And tasted worse.

"I know," Duncan said glumly.

"It must be *really* good for you."

"I sure hope so." He took a breath and downed the rest of it.

How he could without retching, Rose didn't know. The drink left an unfamiliar aftertaste—unfamiliar because Rose wasn't in the habit of eating grass. She scanned the bar for salted peanuts. Rice cakes. Chocolate fudge. Anything.

"It doesn't taste as bad as it smells," Duncan offered, grimacing.

Rose handed him her glass. "Then you may drink mine. Lisa...orange juice, please."

Duncan laughed and set her glass on the counter.

Let him laugh, Rose thought. Orange juice might be plebeian, but it tasted the way juice was supposed to taste.

"Lisa," Duncan said, still laughing, "make that two orange juices."

She'd made him laugh. That was a good sign, Rose decided. But she needed to keep him talking. They needed to bond.

"So tell me about this account that's giving you trouble," she asked after Lisa had set their fresh drinks in front of them.

"I don't want to bore you." Duncan's voice was flat.

As if he could. "But I'm interested," Rose protested. "I'm curious to know what business wouldn't be a success with Burke and Bernard in charge of advertising."

Duncan rested his forearms on the counter and stared into his glass. "Bread Basket Foods."

"The grocery stores?"

Duncan nodded. "Do you shop there?"

"No."

"Neither does the rest of Houston." He heaved a sigh. "And I can't figure it out. Overall, their prices are less than the competition. Focus group after focus group puts cost as the number one factor in choosing where to shop for food. So Bread Basket gives them the best deals in town, yet shoppers stay away."

"Maybe you should advertise differently," Rose suggested, then felt foolish. What did she know? *He* was the professional.

"Did that." Duncan made a sound of disgust and pressed the towel to his face. "I convinced them to double their advertising budget." His voice was muffled until he lowered the towel. "We retooled the campaign and still no corresponding increase in business."

Rose thought about the huge supermarket not too far from her shop. When it had been built several years ago, the Village civic league had protested that the building violated the visual integrity of the neighborhood. After much negotiating, Bread Basket agreed to lower its gaudy sign, but plastic flags, blaring loudspeaker music and a brightly lit parking lot that glowed twenty-four hours a day continued to annoy area residents. "I have to tell you, I wouldn't be sorry to see Bread Basket go out of business."

Duncan looked startled. "Why?"

"I was on the Village Merchants Board when Bread Basket moved in. They managed to alienate everyone. Not too many people living in the Village will support them, but I know most of us have at least gone inside the store. If it were all that great, don't you think we'd shop there?"

"Are you saying there's a boycott?" he asked, looking ready to do battle.

"Nothing official. Everyone is just generally disgusted with them."

Before replying, Duncan took a swallow of juice. "Even with all the hard feelings, I still can't believe there aren't more people who want to save a few dollars."

Rose eyed him. "Do you shop at Bread Basket?"

Duncan shook his head. "No, but I don't shop much anywhere."

"Why not?"

"I—" He broke off and shrugged. "I don't cook very often."

"When you do cook, do you shop at Bread Basket?"

"No." He frowned. "I know where you're going with this, but I'm not the typical Bread Basket customer. Besides, there isn't a store located near me."

"Are the prices of the grocery store where you shop when you do shop lower or higher than Bread Basket's?"

Duncan shifted on the stool and shot her an irritated look. Rose smiled benignly.

"They're somewhat higher," Duncan grudgingly admitted. "I already told you Bread Basket has the best deals in town."

"Yet, according to your focus groups, price is the number one consideration—"

"All right, I already admitted we're in trouble with the account," he grumbled and tossed off the last of his juice. "And I'm not used to failure."

Rose could see that the admission pained him. "I don't think it's your failure. It's Bread Basket's failure."

"What do you mean?"

"I've seen the ads and I could probably even hum the jingle." Rose proceeded to do so, earning a reluctant grin from Duncan. "The truth is, it's too much trouble for me to shop there."

"Why?" Duncan had turned to face her and was regarding her with an intense blue stare. He was listening to everything she said and Rose felt her self-confidence grow. *She* was giving Duncan Burke advice. Who'd have thought it?

"The reason Bread Basket has such great prices is because they sell in bulk. I can't take advantage of that. Where am I supposed to store a case of paper towels or toilet paper? I live by myself. What good does a fifty-pound box of laundry detergent do me? And just picking up a few basics takes forever. Milk is on the far back side. Bread is on the other and there must be a football field of diaper boxes in between."

"That's marketing strategy. The longer you keep customers in a store, the more susceptible they are to impulse buying."

"Whatever." Rose waved away his explanation. "I only know that at the end of a long workday, I just want to pick up a few things and go home. I shop at the Sheffield's near my... boutique."

"Sheffield's is old and out of date, their selection is poor and costs an average of seventeen percent more," Duncan recited. "They've been stagnant for years."

"But I can be in and out of there in five minutes."

There was silence as Duncan weighed her words. "Okay, I'll concede the convenience factor, but not everybody is single like we are," he pointed out. "Bread Basket is targeting families."

Until he mentioned it, the thought that Duncan might have been married had never entered Rose's thoughts. She'd just known that fate wouldn't have sent him to her if he'd been unavailable. "If Bread Basket wants families to shop at their stores, fine. But why did they plop themselves down in the middle of the Rice University area? *Students* live there, for Pete's sake. Whoever selected that site wasn't thinking."

"You're right." Duncan threw up his hands. "And I know you're on target about the rest, too. In fact, I told Bread Basket as much, but they'd gone through two other firms before they came to us. Robert and I thought it would be a challenge." He laughed, but there was no humor in it. "We could just see the headlines." He spread his hands. "Burke and Bernard achieve the impossible. Local agency saves food chain." He winced. "What a mess."

He seemed to find comfort in talking with her and Rose wanted to encourage that feeling. But she knew he didn't have much more time. According to his organizer, the blocked-off time for his class on Thursday nights began at seven-thirty. It was going on six now and he still had to shower and change, eat dinner and drive over to Rice. If Rose could hold his interest, maybe he'd suggest continuing the conversation over dinner.

Racking her brain for some insightful suggestion, she asked, "Is there any possibility Bread Basket would consider changing the way they operate, now that you've tried two different ad campaigns?"

"Ha." Duncan shook his head. "They'll just change agencies. Then whoever they pick will trumpet the fact that they nabbed the account because Burke and Bernard couldn't score.''

Another sports metaphor. She was definitely going to have to take up a sport.

''There will be rejoicing in ad agencies all over Houston,'' he added, patently annoyed by the prospect of losing an account to a competitor.

Rose thought. ''How many other Bread Basket stores are there in Houston?''

''Three. They wanted more but put their expansion plans on hold until these units become profitable. And that appears unlikely no matter what agency they sign with.''

Rose had an idea. She couldn't believe she was going to help Duncan save the much-loathed Bread Basket store that had been an eyesore for five years, but if it would mean working with him, she'd do it.

''I can help you with the Village store.'' She'd caught him glancing at his watch.

''How?'' he asked skeptically.

That touch of skepticism stiffened her backbone. She might not be an advertising professional, but she'd spent her adult life living and working in the Village. Bread Basket had been the topic of a dozen merchant meetings. ''That store has to become more neighborhood oriented. Tell them to remove those tacky flags and stop broadcasting the music in the parking lot.''

The tone in her voice caught his attention. Duncan patted his shorts pocket. ''I need to write this down.''

''Don't bother,'' Rose told him, glad to see he wasn't too vain to listen to her suggestions. ''I won't forget.

We've been pleading with the store management to do those things for five years.''

Duncan reached for the pen Lisa had used and made a note on a napkin. ''But do you seriously think that's all it's going to take to turn that store around?''

Rose shook her head. ''But they have the one thing the Village Association needs desperately: space. Take out one of those diaper aisles and create a community meeting room.''

''They'll never agree,'' Duncan said, but he jotted a note on the napkin anyway. ''That'll kill their profit per square foot.''

''Make up for it with an area for single shoppers.'' Rose visualized her fantasy store. Milk, bread, lettuce and chocolate all within reach. Single-serving meats and frozen dinners close by. ''Gather small-size basics from the other parts of the store and concentrate them in one place. Heavy on the convenience foods. I know they have a high markup. Position the whole thing right by the meeting room.''

Duncan stared at her. ''Because if you're already in the store for a meeting, you'll be more likely to buy a few items on the way out.''

''Exactly.''

A slow smile crept across his face as possibilities occurred to him. ''Rose, you're brilliant! I don't know if they'll go for it, but they'd be crazy not to. I'll pitch it to them myself.'' He slid off the bar stool. ''This is great! *You're* great.'' Leaning forward so quickly Rose had no warning of his intentions, Duncan kissed her soundly on the cheek. ''That's twice you've helped me out of a jam. How am I going to repay you this time?'' Before Rose could suggest dinner, Duncan looked at his watch and made an exclamation. "I've got class tonight. Listen," he said, backing away, "I'll call you—soon!" He blew her a kiss and jogged toward the men's locker room.

Rose was dizzy with delight. Every penny she'd invested in this meeting had been worth it.

Duncan had kissed her! He was going to call her! He—

Still didn't have her phone number.

CHAPTER FIVE

How did Duncan think he was going to contact her if he didn't have her telephone number? Rose only had one telephone number to give him and it was the Rose's Attic number. She didn't bother with a telephone line of her own. She lived in the apartment above her shop and just had an extension phone in her bedroom. She didn't get enough personal calls to make another line worthwhile.

And then Rose realized that Duncan would assume he could call her here, at the hotel. She'd told him she was staying here while she had renovations done. Renovations sounded like a long time. He'd never suspect that she'd only rented the room for one night.

She could always call his office and leave the shop's number, but decided against it. After all her maneuvering, it had become important that Duncan make an effort. And he still could. So for now, she'd give him the benefit of the doubt.

Lisa wiped the counter space next to her. "May I get you anything else?" When Rose shook her head, Lisa discreetly placed the bill for the two orange juices next to Rose's empty glass. "I'll let you total this."

As Rose signed her name, her eyes widened at the amount. Four dollars and fifty cents apiece for two glasses of orange juice? None too generous glasses at that. And Rose belatedly realized she was expected to add a tip and should have added one to the other bill, as well. She included an amount to cover both and resolved to stick with her faux Evian water from now on.

The evening loomed ahead of her. What should she do? Eating alone held no appeal for her. Flexing her arms, she winced and decided that standing under a hot shower or soaking in the tub were her best options. Slipping off the bar stool, Rose returned to her room.

After her shower, she wrapped herself in the hotel's white terry robe, put on her glasses and spread the notes she'd made from Duncan's planner onto the bed. Grabbing an apple from the fruit basket sitting on the minifridge, she crunched into it and studied Duncan's weekly schedule. When would he be most likely to call her?

Thursdays were full with his racquetball and the class he taught. Tomorrow, she'd call Rice and see if there was a course she could take on Thursdays.

Rose placed the pages where she'd re-created his daily schedule side by side.

Most Fridays were blank, except for occasional initials decorating them. Dates, Rose thought. She tortured herself by cross-referencing the initials with the names from his telephone and address section. Patricia Stevens. Kay Hawthorne. Jeanette Deeves. Mary Ellen Bail. Rose had even copied the little notes appearing next to some of those names: December 5, likes roses, size 6—was that a ring size or a dress size? Fitzdonald and Byers, ext. 587.

These people had a life. On a whim, Rose added her name and phone number to the list and noted, "has wedding dress, will marry."

Seeing her name and lonely number next to the others was too depressing. Rose abandoned the initial game and thumbed to her notes on Saturday. "Gym (S. Rod) 8:15," she read. He was going to be at the gym at eight-fifteen on a Saturday night? That didn't make sense. Flipping back through her notes, she saw other "gym" notes. Or was that "sym"? Symphony? That made more sense.

Rose crawled across the bed until she could reach the newspaper on the nightstand. Searching the entertainment section, she found an advertisement for the Houston Symphony featuring pianist Santiago Rodriguez. S. Rod. Without hesitation, Rose picked up the telephone and called the ticket office.

There was good news and bad news. The good news was that there were still tickets available for Saturday night. The bad news was that they were in the expensive front orchestra section. Rose rattled off her credit card information and resolved to starve her body for the next two weeks in order to feed her soul this Saturday.

Okay, she was going to the symphony. She'd never been to the symphony, but knew the fascinating people of Duncan's world attended all the time. And now, just by reciting her credit card number, Rose would be a part of that world, too.

Merciful heavens, what was she going to wear?

"Black," pronounced Connie and Mark in unison.

Rose doubtfully eyed the dress Connie held out. "Okay, black, but maybe a different black?"

"*This* black," Connie insisted, plucking a long-sleeved tent affair from Rose's resisting fingers.

"I'll do your hair in a French twist," Mark decided. "Very sophisticated, with the added benefit of enhancing your bone structure."

Rose had been unaware that she had a bone structure worth enhancing. She touched her cheekbones, sending spasms through her arm muscles. Those, she was aware of.

"And this dress is a rental, not a consignment, so you don't have to feel guilty about borrowing it." Connie removed the dress from the padded hanger. Heavy crepe-backed satin fluttered enticingly.

"But it's a little... bare, don't you think?" Rose pointed to the wide neckline.

"Don't be a prude, Rose." Connie propelled her behind the screen much as she'd had to do with the suit Rose had worn to lunch with Duncan. "Try it on."

That had been Friday when Rose had gone to check on things at the shop. Now it was Saturday evening and Rose was standing in front of the full-length mirror back in her hotel room.

She'd extended her stay in hopes that Duncan would call, but he had not, and Rose was checking out of the hotel tomorrow, no matter what. In the meantime, she was going to the symphony in hopes of encountering him there.

Of course, he probably wouldn't recognize her. She hardly looked like herself. Mark had done her hair in a classic upswept twist. Glittering crystal earrings winked from her earlobes and her shoulders were framed by a low portrait collar. The rest of the dress clung to her, stopping just above her knees.

When she'd originally tried the dress on, Mark had whistled, but it was the look on Connie's face that told Rose she was looking good. Connie was jealous. Of *her*.

Rose pouted her lips at the mirror—her lip muscles being about the only ones not sore—and remembered how Connie had moved closer to Mark and linked her arm through his.

If only Duncan were similarly affected.

Grabbing a beaded evening bag, she headed for the parking garage to retrieve her car. As the attendant drove her valiantly chugging car from the bowels of the hotel lot, Rose reflected that it was time for a new chariot. If Duncan began seeing her on a regular basis, he was bound to notice the car she drove and Rose's car didn't fit the image of a successful woman who wore designer clothes. Too bad she didn't deal in secondhand automobiles.

Jones Hall, home of the Houston Symphony, was located in downtown Houston. The white building with the red-carpeted entrance intimidated Rose at first, but she was soon caught up in the atmosphere of expectation that rippled through the well-dressed crowd.

After searching the foyer and not seeing Duncan, Rose ascended the grand staircase to the mezzanine. Small groups of people stood around drinking coffee, wine and soft drinks. Rose, in order to have an excuse for combing the crowds, ordered sparkling water and moved from group to group casually searching the faces, hoping to make eye contact with Duncan. She didn't see him and positioned herself where she could overlook both the stairs and the entrance. Still no Duncan.

The stairway continued up to the balcony, but Rose didn't think Duncan would have balcony tickets. No, either she'd missed him or he hadn't come tonight.

Deeply disappointed, she started back down to the lower level to find her seat just as the lights flashed and people began entering the rectangular hall.

Rose found her aisle and sat in a spacious plush seat a few rows from the stage. A white-haired gentleman sat on one side of her and a woman sat on the other. Rose nodded to both and noticed that the man's gaze had a disconcerting tendency to linger on her cleavage. She'd *told* Connie the neckline was too low. Now she'd have to remember to sit up straight and hold the program to her chest.

A movement from the box seats on her upper left caught her eye as a dark-haired woman entered, followed by a man.

Duncan.

And he was with someone. Rose's heart began beating faster. The sounds of the tuning orchestra faded away as she stared at the woman. Was this PS? KH? JD? MEB? Or someone else? She was gorgeous and thin and carried herself with confidence. Just the sort of woman who would appeal to Duncan. Just the sort of woman Rose was not.

Rose barely heard the first selection the orchestra played. Time and again, her gaze drifted to the couple in the box. Why did she feel so betrayed? Was it because he'd said he'd call and he hadn't? He hadn't said exactly when he'd call, but he'd said soon. Wasn't two days soon?

The overture ended and the audience stirred as the floor of the orchestra pit was raised and the piano came into view. At another time, Rose might have found all the technical aspects of the performance interesting, but her attention was fixed on two dark heads bent together.

Mechanically, Rose clapped with the audience as a man wearing a red crushed velvet tuxedo jacket strode across the stage to a black concert grand piano.

Rose heard whispering behind her. "He always dresses to match the hall." Rose rather enjoyed the contrast the flamboyantly dressed pianist made next to the somber orchestra.

Once again, her gaze crept to the boxes, but this time, it was intercepted by the white-haired gentleman, who winked at her.

Rose jerked her attention back to the performer on stage and actually managed to forget about Duncan for brief moments during the concerto. But once the lights came up signaling intermission, Rose remembered her goal, scrambled to the aisle and darted up the stairs to the mezzanine.

Sure enough, Duncan and his date were just coming from their box and heading toward the bar. Breathing hard from her dash up the stairs, Rose intercepted them.

"Duncan!" she said, too loudly. Several people, including Duncan and his date, turned to look at her. Rose tried not to pant.

"Hello, Rose." Duncan smiled and waited for her to reach him.

He'd remembered her name. She'd made progress.

"Jeanette—" he turned to the woman at his side "—this is Rose. Rose, Jeanette Deeves."

Jeanette and Rose murmured at each other. Okay, so Duncan only remembered half her name. That was a start.

Jeanette arched a brow inquiringly at Duncan and he started to explain. "Rose is, ah..." Duncan's eyes met hers as he sought for a way to explain their association.

"I was on the Merchants Board for Rice Village and one of Duncan's clients has a store there," Rose inserted, rescuing him. "It has a bit of an image problem, but I'm hoping we can work together to everyone's mutual benefit." This last was a subtle reminder for Duncan.

"That's right." He smiled widely at both of them. "And we were supposed to get together next week and discuss it, weren't we?"

"I don't believe anything definite has been set." This time, her reminder was more pointed.

Rose knew she should say her goodbyes and move on. This was neither the time nor the place to discuss business, but Rose was finding the appropriate times too few and the places too expensive.

"We'll have to get together on that," Duncan said noncommittally and Rose had to be satisfied with that.

"Wasn't the Rachmaninoff magnificent?" Jeanette asked, then laughed. "Though I'd like to drop a few pointers to Mr. Rodriguez's tailor. Did you see that jacket?" She rolled her eyes.

"Oh, don't you know?" Rose asked guilelessly. "He always dresses to match the hall. Red seats, red jacket."

"Hey, I like that." Duncan looked down at Rose approvingly. "Showmanship and the talent to back it up."

Jeanette smiled thinly.

Lines had formed at the refreshment area while they'd stood there. Duncan gestured, indicating that they should move forward. Rose knew she was intruding, knew she should take her leave and walk away, but couldn't think of a casually sophisticated way to do so—and truthfully, didn't try too hard. It was easier just to stay with Duncan and his date.

Jeanette opened her purse and withdrew a pager. After studying it a moment, she sent an apologetic smile toward Duncan. "I've got to call the hospital."

"Go ahead. I'll get your drink for you." As Jeanette hurried toward the public telephones, Duncan explained, "Jeanette's a doctor and she's on call this weekend. In fact," he said, sighing faintly, "she's on call most weekends."

Goody, Rose thought.

"She's very dedicated. Personally, *I* think she works too hard. I'd hoped this evening would be a nice break for her."

Rose did not want to hear any more about Dr. Jeanette. She wanted Duncan to forget all about Dr. Jeanette. That relationship was doomed anyway. Rose was supposed to be Duncan's one true love. When was he going to realize it?

Just two couples stood ahead of them. "Would you care for coffee? Wine or a soft drink?" Duncan offered.

"A soft drink would be lovely, thank you," Rose accepted.

Just then, a breathless Jeanette returned. "Duncan, I am *so* sorry, but one of my patients is having a reaction to some medicine I prescribed." Wearing a pleading expression, Jeanette touched his arm. "Please understand, I've got to go to the hospital."

Duncan gave her a half smile, which told Rose that he and Jeanette had probably been in similar situations in the past. "Don't worry about it. We knew this might happen. After all, that's why we both drove our own cars."

"Thanks," she whispered before standing on her tiptoes and kissing his cheek. Grinning, she wiped away the trace of lipstick, nodded to Rose and slipped away.

"Well." Duncan stepped up to the counter. "I guess that'll have to be *two* colas."

Rose rejoiced. Fate had sent Dr. Jeanette packing. Of course, Rose was sorry about the trouble with the patient, but glad Dr. Jeanette was so dedicated.

"So you're a symphony lover." Duncan handed her a napkin-wrapped glass.

"Yes." At least, she was so far. Rose sipped her drink just as the lights began to flash. "Oh, no." Hadn't intermission just started?

"Don't worry. That's only the first warning. We've got five more minutes." Duncan looked unconcerned, so Rose relaxed and smiled up at him.

She was so happy to be there, standing next to him, surrounded by Houston's classical music lovers. Thanks to Mark and Connie, Rose knew she looked the part of a sophisticated patron of the arts. It was a moment out of one of her fantasies. A handsome man, the plush surroundings, rubbing elbows with Houston's elite—this was a memory she'd always have. Her smile widened in gratitude.

Duncan was in the process of drawing his glass to his lips when he met her eyes. His hand stilled. Unsmiling, he gazed down at her as though reading something unexpected in her expression.

Deep in the back of his eyes, something flickered to life.

Rose caught her breath, too cautious to put a name to the emotion she saw growing there.

His gaze swept the contours of her face, lingering at her lips before he continued bringing the glass to his mouth. He watched her over the rim as he drank.

His expression had never changed, yet Rose knew something was different. It was in the way he looked at her, as though considering her in a context he hadn't thought of before.

The very air was charged with possibilities.

Rose sipped at her cola, the bubbles tickling her tongue as if she were drinking the finest champagne, or the way she imagined they would if she'd ever tasted the finest champagne. She just stopped herself from giggling.

"Are you here by yourself, Rose?" Duncan's voice had a huskiness to it that Rose hadn't remembered being there before.

"Yes," she answered simply.

"Sit the second half with me." It wasn't a request. Rose felt a thrill go through her.

The lights flashed once more. Duncan held out his hand. Rose moved toward him. He took her drink, set it with his on a tray and placed his hand at the small of her back.

Rose wanted to purr. Instead, she used the opportunity to move closer to him—close enough to feel the heat of him through his dark suit jacket. Close enough to see how perfectly she fitted against him. He was just tall enough so her head could rest against his shoulder when they danced.

Just tall enough so that if he bent his head and she tilted hers, their lips would meet.

She shivered.

"Are you cold?" He'd leaned down to speak next to her ear and his breath whispered across her neck and shoulders.

"A little," she said as they sat.

"The air-conditioning can be too enthusiastic on occasion." Duncan took one of her hands and rubbed it between his, then continued holding it as the lights lowered and the orchestra quieted.

Rose would have been content to leave her hand in Duncan's, but clapped with the audience when the conductor strode out and stepped onto the podium. To her disappointment, Duncan didn't reclaim her hand.

Rose wanted to lose herself in dreamy fantasies, but the orchestra wasn't cooperating. Instead of a lush romantic piece with syrupy strings, they were playing a loud, percussive hangover.

The audience was enraptured.

Rose was bored.

Even the knowledge that Duncan was only inches away couldn't prevent her eyelids from drooping. Fortunately, each time she felt herself nod, some instrument would screech or clatter. This wasn't music. This was a train wreck.

Without moving her head, Rose tried to see Duncan out of the corner of her eye. He stared at the stage, one finger pressed alongside his jaw. How could he stand this stuff?

Rose tilted her program, trying to catch the light from the stage so she could read the title of the work. *Moderno 3*. What did that mean?

Moments later, the noise ended, though Rose wondered how anyone knew the piece was genuinely over. But it must be, because the audience was enthusiastically applauding. They were probably glad it was over.

Rose joined them, then, as if responding to someone's signal, people rose to their feet, still applauding.

Duncan was already standing. Belatedly, Rose joined him.

"That was great, just great!" He clapped harder as the conductor returned for a curtain call.

Rose heard shouted bravos and realized Duncan had added his voice to the others. Rose refrained. She'd clapped to be polite. She was standing for the same reason, but she wasn't shouting bravo for something that sounded like the engine of her car when she tried to save money by using a cheaper grade of gasoline.

At last, they could sit down.

"That really gets the blood flowing, doesn't it?" Duncan asked.

"Oh, yes." At least she didn't feel that she was about to fall asleep anymore.

Basking in the good mood of a shared experience, Duncan settled back comfortably and put his arm across the top of Rose's seat. By shifting just inches to the left and leaning back the barest amount, Rose could feel his arm against her neck and shoulders. She sighed.

Duncan must have heard her, for he smiled and cupped his hand around her shoulder as the orchestra began its last selection of the evening.

It was a rare, perfect moment. A lump formed in Rose's throat as she thought how lucky she was to experience the magic. She'd gladly listen to breaking machinery if it inspired this mood in Duncan.

All too soon the concert was over. This time, Rose's applause was genuine in hopes that there might be an encore and a reason to spend more time with Duncan.

The conductor took the podium again and led the orchestra in a rousing John Philip Sousa march that even Rose recognized. Not exactly music for a romantic moment, but it left Rose and the rest of the audience smiling.

"Great concert," Duncan said as they stood. "What did you think of *Moderno 3*?"

Well, I'm not going to be whistling it while I work tomorrow, Rose thought. Duncan very obviously enjoyed it, but it wasn't to Rose's taste. If she were more certain of her herself, she might have told him so, but all this was too new to her. She sought for the right words. "I found it..." What had she found it? Boring and noisy. That didn't sound sophisticated. Remembering an overheard conversation between two of her customers about a piece of artwork, Rose borrowed one of their comments. "I found it intriguingly agitated." Of course, they were talking about art and this was music, but agitation was agitation.

"Yes." Duncan seemed much struck by her observation. "That's it exactly!" He beamed at her. "You intrigue me, too, Rose."

"As long as I don't agitate you."

He laughed. "I don't think there's much chance of that."

They'd moved out of the box and were slowly making their way down the grand staircase, surrounded by chattering symphony patrons.

"Listen, about next week...what do you say we discuss your ideas about Bread Basket over a game of tennis?"

"Tennis?"

He nodded. "Do you play?"

"I love tennis," Rose answered. He was asking her out! He was asking her out!

Duncan smiled with satisfaction. "Let me check my calendar and I'll leave you a message at the hotel."

Rose's heart sank. She wasn't going to be at the hotel, but maybe she could afford to check back in on Thursday and use the gym again. "Yes, do leave a message. I'll be traveling, though." Back to Rose's Attic, but with Houston traffic, that counted in her book.

"One of your buying trips?" Duncan asked.

Rose nodded because it was easier.

"A long one?"

"A couple of days," Rose said. "It depends on what kind of luck I have."

They exited Jones Hall and immediately descended to the underground parking lot. Rose hoped he wouldn't want to walk her to her car. How could she avoid his seeing it this time?

After two flights, they reached her level and Rose paused by the glass doors. "I'm parked on this level."

"I'll see you to—"

"Oh, no," Rose protested. "I'm just over there." She waved her hand in a vague direction, hoping there was a gray car in the vicinity.

"I don't mind," Duncan said, pushing open the door for her, but Rose shook her head.

"Really, go on so you'll beat the worst of the traffic."

"Rose..." Duncan's expression was both determined and puzzled.

She placed her hand on his arm and the door closed once more. "I enjoyed sitting with you. Perhaps we can go to another concert together," she added daringly.

"I'd like that." His voice was quietly sincere and his eyes warmed. He took a step toward her, staying out of the flow of people.

The hurrying crowd and the automobile exhaust fumes evaporated as Rose and Duncan gazed at each other. For just the briefest sparkle of time, Rose thought he might kiss her, then someone pushed by them and Duncan stepped back.

"So I'll see you for tennis on Tuesday or Wednesday?" He opened the door for her and the humid night air swirled around them.

"Sounds great!" Rose injected her voice with enthusiasm. She'd panic later. Just as she stepped onto the oil-stained concrete, she added, as though it were an afterthought and not information her mind had been screaming at her for the past several minutes, "I should warn you, I'm out of practice."

"I'll go easy on you," he called as the door closed between them.

Rose waved and kept the smile on her face until she turned in the direction of her car. *Then* she panicked.

She was out of practice all right. Way out.

The last time she'd held a racquet had been in a summer tennis camp sponsored by the parks department when she was nine years old.

But she should be able to pick up the fundamentals of the game again with a little practice, right?

CHAPTER SIX

WRONG.

"Can't you call this man and just explain that you're rustier than you thought?" an exasperated Connie yelled to Rose from across the public tennis court in Village Park.

"No!" Rose wailed and batted a ball into the net. "This is the first time he's asked me out. If I tell him I can't play tennis, who knows *when* he'll ask me out again?"

Connie trotted to the side and drank from her water jug. Rose hadn't brought one, thinking she'd use the drinking fountain, but apparently, bringing your personal water jug to the court was the chic thing to do. And above all else, Rose wanted to be chic in her dealings with Duncan.

"Who is this guy anyway?" Connie swiped her mouth with her arm.

Decidedly unchic, Rose thought before offering Connie an edited explanation of who Duncan was. "Remember when I looked into advertising for Rose's Attic?"

"Yeah, whatever happened to that?"

Rose had forgotten all about it, that's what. "This is the man I consulted—"

"And now he's dating you!" Connie clapped her hands together. "Way to go. Thank goodness you've dropped Horrible Horace."

"He wasn't horrible," she protested, but was privately amused at Connie's nickname for Rose's erstwhile suitor.

"Yes, he was." Connie picked up her racquet and pointed Rose in the other direction. "Change courts."

"Why?"

"Because that ball you hit into the net was the end of the set."

"So soon?"

"Generally, sets take longer because the other player actually returns the ball and you get into that back-and-forth—" Connie demonstrated with her hands "—kind of thing." She pointed.

Rose looked across to the other court. A group of four kids played doubles. "Well, they've only got to cover half as much area as I do," she protested as she trudged to the other side of the net.

Connie heaved a sigh Rose heard all the way across the court.

It was Sunday afternoon and Connie had good-naturedly responded to Rose's plea for help in polishing up her game. She probably regretted helping her boss on her day off.

"My serve." Connie held up two balls.

"What are you doing?"

"Showing you the balls."

"I *remember* what they look like," Rose said in exasperation.

Connie sagged. "I'm showing them to you because they're new balls. I'm supposed to."

"What am *I* supposed to do?" Too many little details about tennis had escaped her when she was nine.

"All you have to do is hit the ball back to me."

But Rose knew it wasn't that simple. Not only was she supposed to hit the ball, she was supposed to hit it within one of the squares. *That* detail she remembered, for all the good it did her.

Sunday morning, when Rose had checked out of the Post Oak Hotel and made a reservation for Thursday night, she'd discovered that not only would the hotel collect her messages, they were pleased to do so. Apparently, they cultivated repeat guests and Rose's request wasn't all that unusual.

Thus, when she called in Monday morning, it was to find that Duncan had left her a message telling her he had reserved a court time for Wednesday at four-thirty—at the Post Oak Hotel. He liked the late-afternoon time, it seemed, and Rose could see why. He would have completed the bulk of his work by that point in the day. From his planner, Rose knew he was frequently in his office before breakfast. By four-thirty, he was probably tired of doing mental work.

As for the location, Rose hadn't realized there were courts on the hotel grounds. Sighing, she booked a room for Wednesday night there, as well.

On Monday afternoon, Rose went to My Lady Sports at Buffalo Bayou Mall and bought a white tennis outfit with teal trim, matching teal socks, wristbands, new tennis shoes and, only because Mark insisted, a headband. She'd borrowed a racquet from Connie's roommate, so she didn't have that expense, but ended up buying a couple of cans of balls, a thermal water jug in the same teal color, a towel in teal and white and a teal sports bag to carry everything in. Rose blinked twice at the total before silently handing over her credit card. *It's an investment in your future*, she repeated to herself.

On Tuesday morning, Connie's roommate apologetically reclaimed her racquet, so Rose paid a semiprofessional visit to a sports equipment consignment shop and bought a used racquet. The price she paid made her thrifty soul cringe, but at least now, if Duncan asked her to play again, she'd be prepared.

On Tuesday afternoon, the credit card company called to verify that Rose's card hadn't been stolen because there had recently been "unaccustomed activity" on her account. Rose verified all the charges, although it was the first time she'd known the grand total of her campaign to attract Duncan. She decided it was better not to know since she was going to spend the money anyway.

On Tuesday evening, Rose drew out her abused credit card once more and enrolled in a six-week visual arts appreciation course at Rice University. The class met on Thursday nights, but started a half hour before Duncan's class. She'd have preferred that both classes start at the same time, but just getting into a course on the right day was lucky. She'd missed the first meeting, which had been the previous week, but Rose would be able to attend the next five. That ought to allow plenty of opportunities to run into Duncan.

Also on Tuesday, Rose tried to catch up on shop business. She'd virtually abandoned the running of Rose's Attic to Connie, but there were certain decisions Connie couldn't make on her own.

A pile of clothing waited for Rose to decide whether or not she wanted to accept it for consignment or buy it outright for her rentals. And then, too, prom season was coming up and Rose usually advertised in school newspapers in order to boost business. She needed to reserve space and design the ads. Of course, she could use last year's artwork, but by now, she'd hoped to have something catchier.

Duncan could probably whip up a beautiful ad, but now Rose would never ask him. Their relationship was different. Rose had presented herself as a successful businesswoman, which she was, but not on the scale Duncan probably imagined.

And right now, Rose didn't want to explore Duncan's possible reaction to her true circumstances. She had more immediate problems.

She sighed, worrying about the upcoming tennis game. In her mind's eye, Rose could see Duncan playing the racquetball game against his business partner. Duncan went for every ball full out, clearly invigorated by the competition. He hit hard and, by his own admission, wasn't used to losing.

Rose was doomed.

But on the bright side, at least Duncan would win their match.

"How was your trip?" Duncan asked, greeting Rose with a kiss on her cheek.

He'd kissed her! One part of her was thrilled. The other part cautioned her that it was no big deal and she shouldn't treat it as such. Still, she wanted to savor the unexpected embrace, but was too nervous. "I found several prom dresses," she said, glad to be able to tell the complete truth for once. "This is one of my busiest seasons."

"Then I'm doubly lucky you made time for me today."

Rose looked up at the dark-haired man beside her and wanted to melt. *Anytime, anywhere*. She wished she were daring enough to say it aloud.

As they entered the Post Oak Hotel's tennis court area, Rose caught Duncan's appreciative gaze on her.

Thank goodness she'd risked being late and allowed Mark to fix her hair. She'd pulled it into a tight ponytail, but Connie had taken one look and called her boyfriend.

Mark had tut-tutted something about a flat head, which Rose didn't know she had, and gathered her hair loosely, artfully puffing her bangs over the teal headband.

Rose was the epitome of form over substance.

Duncan was form *and* substance. Especially substance. His blinding white tennis shirt and shorts and two sweatbands casually worn on one wrist made Rose's heart thump. At what point should she tell him that he was unlikely to break a sweat in a game with *her*?

She shifted her bag on her shoulder. Maybe if she concentrated on the ball really hard the way Connie had kept telling her to, she might manage a few hits. Duncan had said he'd take it easy on her.

Duncan was making innocuous remarks that Rose had been acknowledging with monosyllables.

"...great racquet. How long have you been playing?"

"Not long." Even though the late-April sunshine was hot, she felt chilled. Connie had been right. Rose should have confessed to Duncan. "You know," she began with a little laugh, "I really don't play all that well."

"Yeah, right." Duncan grinned, his teeth as white as his shirt. "Whenever somebody tells me that, I know I'm about to get the pants beat off me."

While Rose grappled with this image, they dumped their equipment on a bench dividing the two courts. The neighboring court was occupied by another couple. As Rose removed her racquet from the bag, the man stepped behind the woman, held the racquet with her and demonstrated a backhand shot. Over and over, they stepped together. He was teaching her to play tennis. They were standing close together.

What a simple solution. Why hadn't Rose thought to say, I don't play tennis, but I've always wanted to learn? Why don't you teach me a few basics? Men loved to demonstrate their superiority.

Rose wanted to take her racquet and conk herself on the head.

Even that purchase had been ill-advised. Unzipping the cover, Rose could see that by buying a used racquet, Duncan would see the scratches and assume they'd been put there by Rose as she played many hard-fought sets of tennis.

"May I?" He held out his hand for the racquet.

Silently, she handed it to him and watched him test the weight and balance. He batted an imaginary ball and Rose cringed when she heard the air whistling through the strings.

Doomed. She was doomed and no cute tennis outfit would save her.

"Nice." Duncan smiled and handed the racquet back to her, handle first. "That's a serious racquet for a serious player. Don't think you can put anything over on me."

Smiling weakly, Rose took the racquet, noting that the grip was still warm from his hand. Her own hand was stone cold.

Duncan brought out a new can of tennis balls and pulled the ring tab. Rose heard a sucking sound just before she smelled a rubbery odor. This was really happening and she couldn't seem to stop it.

"Heads or tails?" Duncan set his racquet on its head and looked at her.

"Heads?" What was that all about?

Duncan spun the racquet and it fell over onto the green painted surface. "Heads it is," he said and picked it up. "Are you serving or choosing the court?"

"Oh, I'll let you serve first," Rose said, beginning to shake. At this rate, she'd never get the ball over the net.

Turning away from Duncan, she closed her eyes, visualizing Duncan serving the ball and herself returning it. The return didn't even have to be good. She just wanted to get the ball back over the net. *I can do it. I have to,* she told herself as she walked onto the court.

Unfortunately, or perhaps fortunately, Rose concentrated so hard on visualizing her success, she failed to open her eyes. The next thing she knew, the toe of her brand-new, not-yet-broken-in shoes caught on something and she went sprawling facedown onto the court.

"Rose!"

Rose managed to lift her head and turn it in time to see Duncan leap over the net and run toward her. Prone though she was, she could appreciate the sight of him in motion.

He pounded to a stop beside her. "Are you all right?"

"I think so." Other than being completely embarrassed and smudging her outfit, she felt no painful twinges.

"Look at that crack," Duncan said in disgust. He jabbed at it with his foot. "They should maintain these courts better." He knelt down and slid his arms around Rose's shoulders, urging her to sit up.

From her position snug against Duncan's chest, Rose decided she shouldn't be too hasty in proclaiming herself unhurt. Experimentally, she flexed her elbow and brushed off her hands. Duncan captured them in his and turned the palms up. Tiny scratches scored the skin, but only one looked like it might bleed. He brushed at the scratch, sending tingles up her arm.

"You lucked out there," he said, smiling at her.

"Yes," she breathed. "I'm lucky."

His face was so close, she could see each individual eyelash as it framed his blazingly blue eyes, eyes which gazed into hers.

Rose didn't dare move. She wanted nothing to spoil this moment, nothing to end it. She wanted Duncan next to her always. Forever and ever.

The tightness in her chest made it difficult to breathe. Her hammering heart sent tremors through her arms. Could Duncan feel her trembling?

The edge of his mouth curved upward. He raised a hand and caressed her cheek with his knuckles before wiping at her skin with a gentle finger. "You've got some tennis court on your face."

"I'm not surprised." Rose scrubbed at her other cheek.

"So how's the rest of you?" Duncan leaned forward and reached for her ankles.

As he did so, his hair passed right under Rose's nose and she inhaled, capturing the scent, desperately wanting to hold him against her. She wanted to touch him and be touched in return with a such a painful longing that when his hand encircled her ankle, she gasped.

"Did that hurt?" His voice was sharp with concern.

"No." She couldn't lie to him, not about that.

"Are you sure?" With a tenderness that brought a lump to her throat, Duncan explored her ankle with his fingers. "How about here?" He pressed gently, closely watching her face.

"No. Really, I'm fine."

"Let's make certain. Do you want to try to stand?"

Rose nodded and Duncan slid his arm around her waist. She clutched his shoulder and pretended the circumstances were different and that he was truly sweeping her off her feet.

He was solid and safe and Rose felt very feminine. She liked being in his arms and wanted to prolong the moment.

"Put weight on that foot gradually," Duncan instructed when she was upright.

He did say gradually, Rose reminded herself as she slowly—and very reluctantly—relinquished her hold on him. He kept his arm around her waist, shifting his hand.

An aching grew in her middle as her body responded to his touch. Why couldn't she just kiss the man and get it over with? Why couldn't the time be right?

When *would* the time be right?

She'd never felt this way before, certainly not with Horrible Horace. His end-of-date kisses she endured, hoping they'd get better. With Duncan, Rose wanted to skip the date and get right to the kisses.

Unfortunately, there'd hardly be any chance of that after they started playing tennis. He'd be frustrated and annoyed with her, emotions not conducive to kissing.

As she put full weight on her foot, his hands fell away. She wanted them back.

"Okay?" he asked.

"Mmm." She could barely make a sound and she didn't trust herself to meet his eyes.

"Now, try walking."

He took her arm at the exact moment Rose stepped forward. The unexpected contact made her inhale softly.

"I *knew* it. You are *not* all right, but you get points for pretending you are."

"Duncan, really—"

"No arguing." He draped her arm over his shoulders and helped her to the bench. "And no tennis for you today."

"No tennis?"

"Absolutely not."

No tennis!

Rose started limping. Fate had intervened once again, though it had taken Rose a few minutes to recognize the opportunity.

Duncan saw that she was seated on the bench, then gathered their assorted equipment, slung both sports bags over his broad shoulders and held out his hand to Rose.

Rose concentrated on remembering which foot she should be limping on.

"I'm going to speak to the hotel manager about the deplorable condition of the courts," Duncan vowed.

Rose kept quiet. She *had* fallen. Though she wasn't truly hurt, someone else could be. "There has been some rain recently. They might not be aware of the crack."

"They're lucky you're the one who fell." Duncan gave her shoulders a squeeze. "Anyone else would have already called a lawyer."

"Accidents happen," Rose said.

"I wish more people felt as you do." Duncan's voice was warm with approval.

As soon as they entered the side lobby of the hotel, the concierge hurried from behind his station. One look at Duncan's face and the man began to babble. "May I be of assistance?"

"Ms. Franklin tripped over a crack in the tennis court," Duncan snapped, leaving little doubt that he held the hotel completely responsible. "Is the hotel doctor available?"

"Oh, Duncan, please." Rose was both appalled at the way things were snowballing out of control and thrilled with the respect Duncan commanded.

He gazed down at her, all stern and manly. "Rose, let me handle this."

So she did.

With Duncan's help, she limped her way into one of the hotel offices for privacy. To her relief, the hotel doctor was gone for the day, which prompted several pithy comments from Duncan.

Still muttering, he knelt at her feet, a position Rose found appealingly fraught with symbolism, and gingerly pulled back her teal sock.

He sucked air between his teeth. "It's already starting to turn color. Where's that ice?" he barked at the concierge. The man had disappeared. "Hang tight and I'll see what's keeping him. Why don't you loosen the laces on your shoe?"

As soon as Duncan was out the door, Rose examined her foot. It didn't hurt, but maybe she'd injured herself after all. She took off her shoe and pulled down her sock to reveal her greenish foot.

The sock. Dye from her new socks had stained her foot—and the inside of her shoe, as well, she discovered when she checked. Great. She put the shoe back on. The socks had been expensive, but they'd matched the trim on her tennis outfit, so she'd bought them. She should've washed them before she'd worn them.

"Here we go." Duncan reappeared, wrapping a towel around a bag of crushed ice. "I got this from the bartender. The concierge is hunting down the first-aid kit." He knelt and gently placed the makeshift ice bag on her foot. "How's that? Does it hurt?"

"I don't feel anything," Rose said truthfully.

Duncan grimaced. "That'll come later. Believe me, I know." He rose and dragged a wheeled secretary's chair over to sit beside her.

"You've had a lot of sports injuries?" Rose asked, trying to get the subject away from her perfectly fine, though greenish, foot.

Duncan stretched out his legs and pointed to a white line with stitch marks on either side of it. "That one was the worst. Popped a tendon in college and had to have surgery." He smiled at her. "Probably kept me from doing something stupid, like going pro."

"Were you disappointed?"

"Not for long." His gaze shifted to someone behind her. "And here comes the Ace bandage, if I'm not mistaken."

The concierge handed Duncan several packages. "This is the selection from our pro shop," he explained. "I hope one will suffice."

"This'll be fine." Duncan was already ripping open a package. He indicated that Rose should lay her leg across his. "I may not be a doctor, but I've wrapped my share of ankles."

The concierge gathered the rejected bandages and withdrew, much to Rose's relief. "I think you're making a lot of unnecessary fuss," she told Duncan as he removed her shoe. Though he didn't even glance at it, Rose tipped it over so the inside wouldn't show.

"Yes and no," he said. "You can bet that crack in the courts will be repaired by tomorrow." He worked swiftly, and within moments, Rose's foot was wrapped in a flesh-colored stretchy bandage. "Try that out."

Rose stood. "It feels fine." As though it wouldn't. Guilt and relief at escaping the tennis game were warring for Rose's chief emotion at the moment. Guilt was winning.

"Fortunately, there isn't much swelling." Duncan collected the ice and stood, too. "How about some dinner? As I recall, we were going to discuss the Bread Basket store today."

"Dinner," Rose said firmly, "sounds like a wonderful idea."

*   *   *

Dinner turned out to be more than just a wonderful idea. It was magical. Still dressed in their tennis clothes, Rose and Duncan went to the hotel restaurant and talked about everything *but* the Bread Basket grocery store. And the more they talked, the more firmly convinced Rose became that Duncan was her destiny.

She tried to pinpoint exactly the precise moment when her feelings crystallized into love and realized that she'd been in love since the first moment she'd seen him.

Logically, she shouldn't believe in love at first sight. Not true love. Love should grow after getting to know someone. But when Duncan laughed at something she said or his eyes lit with enthusiasm over a point with which they were in agreement, Rose couldn't imagine loving him any more than she already did—and had since that first moment. They were meant to be together forever and ever. And that was that.

Shyly, Rose told Duncan about the arts appreciation course she planned on taking at Rice. At least he wouldn't be surprised when he saw her there.

"I teach a marketing course at Rice on Thursday nights," he mentioned, as she suspected he would. "It keeps me on my toes and lets me check out all the bright future account executives."

"Your competition?" Rose asked.

Duncan laughed. "Only if I don't hire them first."

Rose couldn't imagine why anyone would want to work elsewhere.

"So, you're going to learn to appreciate art?" Duncan asked.

"I'd like to know more about it and the artists themselves." Which was true. She also wanted to learn enough to intelligently converse on the subject. She could just imagine attending small elegant gatherings with Duncan's friends. People like that talked about art, didn't they?

Duncan caught their waiter's eye. "Coffee? Cappuccino?" he asked Rose.

Rose had been about to decline the coffee, but opted for the cappuccino. She knew what the frothy milk-topped drink was, of course, but she'd never ordered it. Tonight, she would.

"I've found artists very... arty," Duncan said with a laugh.

"What do you mean?" Rose asked.

"Oh, you know... that whole crowd on the circuit."

What circuit? As Rose tried to figure out what on earth Duncan was referring to, the waiter brought their cappuccinos. "Oh, it smells so good!" Rose exclaimed. Closing her eyes, she inhaled the aroma again.

"That's what I like about you, Rose," Duncan said, his voice quietly sincere. "You're not jaded. You're not afraid to enjoy the simple things. When I'm with you, I enjoy them more, too." He reached across the table and covered her hand with his. "Don't ever change."

CHAPTER SEVEN

"ROSE!" Duncan hailed her from across the campus courtyard.

"Duncan?" It was after seven, so he was running late. That wasn't like him. Rose stopped walking until he caught up with her.

He looked wonderful, though rushed. And as always, the very air around him seemed to vibrate with energy and excitement. With *life*. And she felt more alive just being in his presence.

"How's the ankle?" he asked, kneeling down to see it.

"Fine." She'd wrapped it, however, in case she saw him after class this evening. He'd cautioned her to err on the side of overprotectiveness and it was easier to wrap the ankle than argue with him. "Feels like I never hurt it at all," she added. Holding out her foot, she wiggled it in all directions.

"Excellent movement. You're a fast healer."

"I guess so," Rose mumbled as he stood. "Duncan? Wasn't your class supposed to start twenty minutes ago?"

"Yes." He snatched a quick glance at his watch. "My car battery died. I replaced it three months ago, which means something's probably wrong with the car's electrical system. Anyway, I *am* late, but I wanted to ask you if you were going to the Janeway Gallery showing on Saturday."

Rose knew nothing of the Janeway Gallery showing. "I hadn't planned to."

Duncan grimaced. "Yeah, I hate those charity things, too, but Burke and Bernard donated the invitation design and I feel I ought to show up. Come with me?"

"Yes. I'd love to." No treacherous waters to navigate here.

"Great! It'll be a chance for me to introduce you to some of my friends." He jogged backward. "I'll call you!"

Rose's smile froze. *Meet some of his friends?* Panic set in. She wasn't ready to meet his friends. What would they think of her? What would they think of *him* for bringing her? What if she said something stupid?

Wouldn't Duncan wonder why no one knew her—why no one had ever seen her at one of their gatherings?

What if they didn't like her?

Or worse, what if someone recognized her as unassuming Rose of the secondhand clothing store?

Blindly, Rose walked to her classroom where, to her surprise, she managed to subdue her panic long enough to lose herself in her instructor's art lecture. The class had begun with a discussion of ancient classics, which she'd missed, and was moving chronologically through the ages to encompass modern art.

It was all new and wonderfully interesting to Rose. Why hadn't she ever signed up for these continuing education classes before? There were ones offered on music and literature, as well, and Rose vowed to take them all.

She'd become so fascinating that Duncan—and his friends—would be fascinated, too.

Too bad she couldn't cram all the courses in before Saturday night.

Rose didn't sleep well Friday night, even though she was back in her own bed. Tonight was the night. Tonight, Duncan would introduce her to his friends and Rose would officially become part of his world.

She was alternately thrilled and terrified.

"Got a date? You've been hanging around the designer racks for half an hour," Connie said from behind the counter.

"Yes, sort of." Why did everything have beads on it? Rose didn't want to wear beads. She didn't feel glittery. Besides, beads would make her stand out and she wanted to blend in.

"What is it this time—a polo match?"

"Very funny," Rose said over her shoulder. Connie thought the story of Rose's "sprained" ankle was hilarious and refused to believe Rose hadn't planned it from the very start.

"So tell me where you're going."

Rose sighed and reached for the black number she'd worn to the symphony. "Some art show at the Janeway Gallery."

A book dropped. "You're kidding!"

Connie sounded so astonished, Rose turned to face her. "No, why?"

"That's a hoity-toity charity affair."

"I was hoping it was a small, casual charity affair." She was going to be sick.

"Not a chance. Attended by the crème de la crème. The crustiest of the upper crust." Connie abandoned her books and came out from behind the counter. "Put that black dress back. He's already seen it and you need something different."

Chiffon fluttered as Rose moved down the racks.

"And don't bring out that black sack, either," Connie warned without even looking at her. How did she know Rose was thinking of that dress? "You need something distinctive and arty because you don't have real jewels."

"I'll just wear some of the crystal. It's a good quality." Besides, there was a pair of dangling earrings Rose had secretly been longing to wear.

"Rose, you are hopeless." Connie pulled out a silk brocade mother-of-the-bride-type suit, sighed heavily and put it back. "You can't wear fake jewelry in that crowd. They know the difference. They *own* the difference. That's why you have to go a little funky."

"I'm not a funky person," Rose said, knowing it wasn't going to make any difference whatsoever.

"There's *nothing* here." Connie dismissed the shop's entire inventory. "Maybe we could borrow—wait a minute!" She grinned, looking enormously pleased with herself. "I've got it, I've got it!" She scampered up the stairs through the loft.

"Connie, I only store the Halloween costumes up there," Rose called after her.

"I know." Connie's voice was gleeful, though muffled.

Rose didn't have time to humor Connie. She had to call the hotel and check for Duncan's message. As she dialed the number of the reception desk, Rose wondered if Duncan thought it curious that she was never there when he called.

"Yes, Ms. Franklin, Mr. Burke requests that you call him at your earliest convenience. He left this number."

Rose copied it down and thanked the receptionist. She didn't recognize the telephone number. She'd memorized his personal one and the Burke and Bernard switchboard number.

Instead of calling Duncan at once, Rose got out her notes from his planner to investigate.

Mechanic. This was the telephone number of Duncan's mechanic. Rose had a bad feeling, which was confirmed by an apologetic Duncan.

"Rose, a short took out the whole electrical system in my car. It won't be fixed until Tuesday. Could I beg a favor?"

She knew what was coming. "Sure."

"I hate to do this to you, but could you drive tonight?"

Tell him you're sick. Laugh and say, "Oh, what a co-incidence, my car is in the shop, too!" It probably ought to be anyway. Tell him you'll see him another time. Tell him— "What time shall I pick you up?"

Duncan gave her careful directions to his house in West University, a stylish area populated by young professionals. "About eight-thirty? I'll be watching for you."

Rose quietly hung up the telephone and covered her mouth with her hands. This was disaster.

"Rose, look what I—what's wrong?" Connie's concerned face peered over the loft banister. "Did he weasel out on you?"

Slowly, Rose lowered her hands. "No. He's got car trouble and wants me to drive tonight."

"Oh. What's wrong with that?"

"What's wrong with *that*?" Rose could hear her voice crescendoing into a shriek. "You've seen my car...I can't drive it to a 'hoity-toity' charity event."

"Then hire a limousine. That would be fun."

"We're not high schoolers going to the prom!"

"Then rent a car," Connie said and disappeared again.

Rent a car. So simple. Rose calmed down.

Except that Duncan thought she drove a gray Mercedes.

Okay, then Rose would rent a gray Mercedes.

"I still think the cigarette holder would be the perfect touch," Connie insisted. "Why won't you carry it?"

"Because I don't smoke," Rose countered just as stubbornly. She wasn't even sure she could pull off the outfit Connie had assembled for her, but there wasn't time to find another one.

Rose had spent all afternoon trying to find a charcoal gray Mercedes she could rent. She'd finally settled for one more silver than charcoal, and hoped the night would camouflage the lighter color.

Her credit card took another hit, but again Rose told herself it was worth it.

"Close your eyes, hon. I'm going to spray," Mark said.

Rose closed her heavily made-up eyes. "I'm not sure about this," she said and got a mouthful of hair spray.

"Trust me," Mark said and stuck a chopstick in her hair. "Did I give you some of my business cards?"

"Yes," Rose replied. "But I could use more." She'd left them all over the Post Oak Hotel, but had never actually given them to anyone.

"I knew it!" Mark shot a triumphant glance at Connie, who returned it adoringly. "People are beginning to *notice*."

Rose tried not to think about the concept of her head attracting attention.

"Which earrings?" Connie held up some jade drops and a pair of miniature paper lanterns.

"I'll wear the jade," Rose said firmly.

"Oh, but the lanterns are so cute."

"I'm already having trouble with the chopsticks." Mark had done her hair in stacked loops reminiscent of a geisha. Her face was powdered into a pale mask with cherry red lips and black-rimmed eyes.

"You're absolutely right about the cigarette holder. It doesn't go," Connie said.

Rose met her eyes in the mirror. "You're trying to distract me from the real issue, which is that I look like I'm going to a Halloween party!"

A look passed between Mark and Connie. Silently, Connie handed Rose the jade drop earrings. "We could tone down your eye makeup, but really, Rose, it only looks strange to you because you're not used to wearing that much."

Rose whisked off the towel Mark used to protect her clothes. "I don't have time. I don't want to be late picking up Duncan." She stood.

"Wait." Mark repositioned the towel. "Close your eyes." He brushed at Rose's face with the soft powder brush. "How's that?"

More of Rose's natural color showed through the powder and she didn't look quite so costume-y. Connie's find in the loft was a flowing kimono in a bright print that Rose wore open over black trousers and top, with the obi sash at her waist. She looked ... arty.

"Thanks, you guys." She smiled.

"No problemo." Mark pressed his business cards into her hand.

The Mercedes drove like a dream and Rose easily found Duncan's single-story contemporary house.

He was waiting for her when she drove up a few minutes before the agreed-upon time, so Rose only caught a quick impression of other contemporary-style houses, well-kept lawns and a number of joggers.

"You're prompt," he said, buckling his seat belt. He wore a dark jacket, collarless shirt and a devastating smile. "I like that in a person."

Rose simply gazed at him, breathing in the faint citrus scent from his shaving soap.

"Did you want me to drive?" he asked when she didn't move.

Flustered at being caught staring, Rose stammered, "D-do you prefer to?"

"I wouldn't mind trying out this model," he said. "I've just about had it with my car." After they changed places and Duncan pulled away from the curb, he commented, "You've put a lot of miles on this car."

"It doesn't seem that way," Rose said rather desperately, and gazed out the window.

"That's a good sign," Duncan said.

"I guess it is." She turned back to him, determined to change the subject. "So how's the new Bread Basket campaign coming? Have you convinced them they need to change their image?"

"I wouldn't talk to them before running everything by you," Duncan told her. They'd come to a stop sign and he gave her a warm smile before driving on.

Rose was elated. He valued her opinion! She could hardly believe it.

"Robert and I are taking our time. We want everything nailed down before we present the campaign." He signaled and merged onto the freeway. "No one is going to accuse Burke and Bernard of running scared."

Rose had picked the right subject to discuss. It lasted the entire drive to the gallery and kept her from dwelling on the fact that soon she would be meeting Duncan's friends.

Her nerves caught up with her the instant Duncan dropped the keys into the valet's hand.

Light spilled from a gray stone house in the museum district. Once homes of the wealthy, most houses in the area were now converted into trendy bistros, bed and breakfasts, galleries and the offices of architects and lawyers.

Rose climbed the steps with Duncan, her anxiety increasing at each level.

Duncan leaned close as they entered the gallery. "By the way, you look great," he murmured, just when Rose's confidence was flagging.

She was traveling into a completely different world and Duncan was her passport. He also became her tour guide and translator.

"Duncan!" A bejeweled older woman wearing black hailed him.

"Maude!"

An air kiss followed.

Rose tried not to stare at the enormous stone on Maude's finger.

"Do you know Rose Franklin?" Duncan inquired.

"I don't believe so." The woman shifted her attention to Rose.

Though Rose felt defensive, there was nothing in the woman's attitude to make her feel that way. She relaxed the tiniest bit. Before she could say anything, the crowd closed around them and Maude's attention was captured by new arrivals.

"Duncan!" Another woman, another black dress and more jewels.

"Cece!"

Another air kiss.

"I didn't know you were back in the country." Duncan turned to Rose. "Do you know Rose?"

"I'm Rose Franklin," Rose said, sidestepping the question altogether.

Cece put one jeweled finger up to her mouth. "Are you Buzz Franklin's new daughter-in-law?"

"Cece, a married woman? You wound me!" Duncan slipped his arm around Rose's waist.

Cece leaned toward Rose. "Duncan's a rogue, but we love him anyway." With a coy laugh at Duncan, Cece wandered to the next chatting group.

"A rogue, hmm?" When Rose glanced up at Duncan, she noticed an interesting stain on his cheekbones.

"Cece exaggerates," he said repressively.

With his hand firmly in the small of her back, Duncan steered Rose toward a group of men and women about their own ages.

"Duncan!" This time, the woman did not wear black and was not wearing jewels. Silver dolphin earrings leaped through her earlobes. Attired in jeans, a rain forest awareness T-shirt and a jacket, her only other piece of jewelry was a button that read, "No animal products were used in the manufacture of this garment."

"Good to see you, Ginger."

No air kiss here. Duncan kissed Ginger on the cheek just the way he'd kissed Rose that time he'd greeted her.

A little pang shot through her.

"Hello, Rose," a male voice sounded next to her.

"Robert!" Grateful to find a familiar face in the crowd, Rose smiled with genuine pleasure and raised her cheek when she saw Duncan's partner bending his head.

Okay, social kissing was the rule in this crowd. She'd have to remember that in future meetings with Duncan, she thought, eyeing him as he greeted the others. No sense in wasting opportunities.

Checking out what the other women were wearing, Rose could see that Connie had been absolutely on the mark in outfitting her. It was either real jewels or nothing. A look Rose dubbed "environmental activist" was popular, along with several ethnic ensembles. One woman wore a turban. Two model types wore short, tight dresses that real people couldn't wear, so Rose didn't count them.

The fact that both Duncan and Robert knew her granted Rose an immediate and casual acceptance into the crowd. Rather than addressing her as a newcomer, the others continued talking, obviously assuming she knew what and whom they were discussing.

Rose laughed when everyone laughed and nodded when everyone nodded.

And the entire time, she was terrified she'd be exposed as an interloper.

Conversations eddied around her and Rose wanted to try wading in, but couldn't find a topic to float. The gentle pressure of Duncan's hand at her waist caused her to look up at him.

"Would you like to meet one of the artists?" he asked in an undertone.

Rose was grateful to be rescued. "Yes, I would."

Duncan nudged her in the direction of a man standing next to three paintings. Long-haired and bearded, he was dressed in baggy black with a white T-shirt and paint-spattered tennis shoes.

"Are those his paintings?" she asked, hoping they weren't.

"I imagine so. I remember them from the brochure we did."

"Oh."

A corner of Duncan's mouth quirked in amusement. "So... what do you think?"

Rose had been scouring her mind for a comment, desperately wishing that her art course had begun in the present and worked toward the past. "I think I'd like to take a closer look." And buy time in the process.

The three wall-size paintings were variations on a theme. Bright colors swirling in a sea of red filled the canvas except for a white area at the top. Near the bottom corner, a chunk of the canvas had been torn off and the painting was "leaking" down the wall and puddling onto the floor.

"He painted the wall and the floor," Rose murmured, wondering what the gallery owner thought of it all.

"Yes, he did." Duncan clasped his hands behind his back as they stood and regarded the paintings.

Rose hadn't meant Duncan to hear her comment. The only comments she wanted him to hear were witty, insightful ones. She wished she knew what he was thinking. She already knew he liked modern music; he probably liked modern art, as well.

But did he like this particular piece of modern art? Without moving her head, she swiveled her eyes and tried to gauge his reaction to the paintings. Inspiration struck. "What do the paintings say to you?"

Duncan regarded her a moment before replying. "The artist feels that the commercialism of society is draining away his creativity."

How on earth did Duncan get *that* from the painting? "Does he?"

"Oh, yes. Although he despises himself for it, Trey—" Duncan gestured toward the young man "—free-lances for the agency when he needs to buy groceries. Fortunately for us, he eats on a fairly regular basis."

"But why does he dislike working for you?"

"We 'revel in crass commercialism'."

All was now clear to Rose. "And that's his statement."

"You got it." Duncan urged her forward and introduced her to Trey.

"My, my, Duncan." The artist took her hand and looked soulfully into her eyes. "'A lovely being, scarcely form'd or moulded, A rose with all its sweetest leaves yet folded.'" He bowed over her hand and kissed her fingers.

"I beg your pardon?" Rose pulled at her hand.

The look Trey gave her was punctuated by a contemptuous arch of his eyebrow. "I was quoting Byron. I assumed you'd recognize it," he said with a dismissing smile that set Rose's cheeks flaming.

Beside her, she felt Duncan tense. She'd exposed her ignorance, but perhaps she could make up for it by commenting on the paintings. "I'm sorry you're feeling drained," she blurted out.

Trey, who had already turned away from them, looked back. "Drained?"

"Yes. Your creativity." She pointed to the puddle on the floor. "I hope you get it back."

Trey blinked.

Duncan coughed. "I think Rose and I will find something to drink."

There was no mistaking the urgency with which Duncan maneuvered Rose through the crowd. When he grabbed two glasses of champagne from the refreshment table and kept going, she knew she was in trouble.

Why hadn't she kept her mouth shut? Obviously, she'd said the wrong thing and Duncan was taking her away before she could embarrass him further.

Meekly, she followed as he led her into the back part of the gallery.

"Let's go out into the sculpture garden." Duncan handed Rose one of the glasses and shouldered open a door.

Humidity enveloped her and fogged her glass as Rose stepped onto a small patio ringed with unidentifiable stone and metal shapes.

"This way." Duncan followed a pebbled path that led to a shrub-surrounded concrete bench. "Great. Nobody else is out here yet." He brushed at the bench and indicated that she should sit.

Feeling miserable, Rose sat and swiveled to face him. "Duncan—"

"Shh." He interrupted her apology by placing a finger against her lips. "You are incredible."

"I am?" And he didn't make being incredible sound like a bad thing.

"His face!" Duncan started laughing. "Did you see Trey's face when you told him you hoped he got his creativity back?"

She'd been trying to sympathize with the artist and to let him know she understood his work. Obviously, her words had been interpreted differently.

"You skewered him but good and he deserved it. I was ready to strangle him when he pulled his superiority act with you." Duncan laughed again. "But you can take care of yourself, can't you?"

"Not all the time," Rose said, still trying to understand exactly what had happened. She took a sip of the champagne. It was warm, so she set it on the bench beside her.

"I have never held with pretentious people and Trey is one of the worst." Duncan tasted his champagne, grimaced and held out his hand for Rose's glass.

"I thought Trey worked for you." When Rose handed over her glass, Duncan unceremoniously dumped the contents of both into the azaleas.

"He does. I like his work, but I don't like him."

Rose sagged with relief. She'd been so afraid that Duncan was angry with her but, miracle of miracles, she'd once again inadvertently stumbled onto the right thing to say. The stress was getting to her.

"He's a hypocrite, but he's a talented hypocrite," Duncan was saying. "On the other hand, I'm sick of his lectures. I'm sick of the way everyone fawns all over him—Rose what's the matter?"

She put a hand to her temple and forced her breathing to slow. "I thought you were angry with me because I'd insulted one of your friends."

"Angry?" He gazed down at her, his eyes the darkest blue she'd ever seen them. "I'm not angry. In fact, I..." He tilted his head inches closer to hers and stopped. "I think you're a very special person."

"You do?"

Duncan curved his fingers around the side of her neck, caressing her jaw with his thumb. "I do," he whispered, then kissed her.

It was a firm but restrained kiss. Very pleasant as kisses went, hinting at a deeper passion that could be invoked under the right circumstances. A very proper first kiss, especially since they were at a public gathering and someone could wander into the sculpture garden at any moment.

But Rose had been hoping for a rocket-launching, stars-bursting sort of kiss. She was ready for a rocket-launching, stars-bursting kiss.

She *wanted* a rocket-launching, stars-bursting kiss.

Duncan pulled back to gaze at her. "You are so sweet," he murmured.

"I," said Rose, "wish to be something else." Placing a hand on either side of Duncan's very broad shoulders, she parted her lips and jerked him toward her.

Rose's approach may have lacked finesse, but Duncan responded immediately, capturing her mouth with his. His arms tightened around her and he deepened the kiss. Cupping her head with his hand, he moved his mouth over hers, breathing something Rose couldn't hear because of the noise from the rockets being launched.

A thousand stars burst and Rose wanted to laugh with the sheer joy of it all. Instead, she burrowed her hands beneath his jacket, exploring the muscles she'd seen at the gym, feeling them move as his hands splayed against her back. She scooted closer, trying to press as much of her body against his as she could. She belonged there, next to him. She could feel the rightness of it.

"Rose." His breathing ragged, Duncan lifted his mouth from hers and nuzzled her neck before trailing urgent kisses back to her lips. "*Rose.*"

The back door of the gallery opened, sending light and laughter toward them, intruding on the world they'd created.

Drawing a shuddering breath, Duncan opened his eyes and stared at her. He looked stunned, the same kind of stunned Rose felt that first moment she'd seen him. "Rose?"

"Yes, Duncan?" She understood. He had only just now realized what she'd known from the first: They were meant to be. Always. Forever.

Soon.

His arms still encircled her and she set her cheek against his chest, smiling at the thundering of his heart.

He cleared his throat. "Rose, it's time you met my parents."

CHAPTER EIGHT

A PROPER note from Duncan's mother was waiting for Rose when she checked into the Post Oak Hotel the following Thursday for her usual workout.

She raced to her room, ripped open the heavy cream envelope and ran her fingers over the engraved monogram.

Heavy cream paper and engraving naturally led to thoughts of weddings. Rose sighed, then unfolded the note. Duncan's mother wrote that she was looking forward to meeting Rose and having her stay with them the weekend of the eighteenth. She signed it "Nadine Burke" in bold, no-nonsense handwriting.

Stay an entire weekend? At the most, Rose had expected a dinner invitation or maybe a Sunday afternoon visit. A whole weekend with Duncan and his parents. This was serious. Sinking onto the bed, Rose stared at the note from Duncan's mother. Two weeks. Rose was going to meet Duncan's parents in a little over two weeks.

When Duncan mentioned meeting them, Rose was certain he'd forget. After all, she herself had trouble remembering any details of their evening together after he'd kissed her.

Gallery guests had wandered into the sculpture garden and she and Duncan had returned to the front rooms. He'd stayed by her side, possessively linking their hands together when the crowd threatened to separate them.

120

Rose spoke to people, she must have, but after a span of time she couldn't begin to judge, her eyes had met his and held. Moving as one, they'd set their glasses on a window ledge and left the gallery.

The drive to Duncan's home was silent—or they could have talked nonstop. Rose couldn't remember. What she did remember was Duncan parking the car and taking her into his arms once again. She hadn't wanted to leave, but Duncan had gently sent her on her way. Then he stood at the curb watching until she drove out of sight.

The evening had been so romantic. Rose heaved a great sigh and fell back onto the bed, the note from Duncan's mother clutched to her chest. When a man asked a woman to meet his parents, his intentions were serious. Duncan, in his take-charge manner, was moving things right along.

In fact, Rose wondered what had taken him so long to recognize the inevitable. *Rose Burke*. Not bad, but rather unmusical, unlike Mrs. Duncan Burke, which fairly flowed from the tongue.

What kind of people were his parents? Was it from his father that he inherited those blue, blue eyes and the heavy black brows? And his self-confident personality, did that come from his mother? She could hardly wait to meet the two people whose love had produced Duncan. She already knew she'd love them, too.

A shadow fell over the happy scene in Rose's mind. She sat bolt upright, the first icy fingers of dread squeezing her heart. Duncan would want his parents to approve of her, but what if they were a little slow to realize that Duncan and Rose were meant for each other?

They'd be cautious and testing. They'd want to be certain Rose was worthy of their son. Duncan obviously loved his parents and respected their opinion. And didn't Rose want that opinion to be a positive one?

Meeting Duncan's parents was a test. She'd better start studying.

Duncan was pleased when Rose told him about the invitation she'd received. "Mom's obviously impatient, but I wanted to wait until we got the Bread Basket campaign out of the way. Are you free that weekend?" He leaned over to check the control panel on her stationary bike. "Let's up the resistance a notch." He proceeded to do so and Rose felt the difference immediately. So did her leg muscles.

"Yes, I'm...free that weekend." She tried not to pant.

"My parents will adore you." With an adoring look of his own, he tucked one of Mark's artfully arranged tendrils behind her ear.

At the touch of his fingers, Rose shivered.

Just then, Duncan's racquetball partner emerged from the locker room and touched his elbow. Duncan nodded to him. "Time for my game." He hesitated. "Listen, Rose, don't feel neglected if a couple of days go by and I haven't called you. I work long and crazy hours pulling everything together at the end of a campaign."

Her heart sank. "Of course. Don't worry about me. This is my busy season, too."

Duncan gave her an intimate smile. "I knew you'd understand." He dropped a kiss on her forehead and followed his partner across the gym. "I *will* be thinking of you."

"Me, too." Watching until he entered the court area, Rose stopped pedaling and let the momentum of the bike move her legs. Then she readjusted the resistance.

She was disappointed that he'd be so involved with his business they wouldn't be seeing each other, then decided it would be an excellent opportunity to demonstrate that she wasn't one of those pouting, clinging females who demanded attention all the time. Duncan would hate that sort of woman, Rose sensed.

It would be hard not to be with him, though. Not when she thought about him day and night. Rose grabbed her water bottle and drank deeply before leaving the exercise bicycle and approaching another machine.

Duncan had said that his mother was impatient; that was a good sign. Obviously, he'd told her about Rose and it meant Mrs. Burke wanted to meet her as soon as possible. If Rose hadn't had her arms occupied with weights, she would have hugged herself. She suspected that Duncan didn't often bring women to meet his parents. Anyway, she didn't want to think about Duncan with other women. They weren't important anymore now that Rose was in his life.

Which reminded her, if she wanted to stay in his life, she had a lot of work to do.

During the next week while Duncan toiled on the final details of the Bread Basket campaign, Rose practically lived at the library.

She checked out books on etiquette, Shakespeare and Lord Byron. She read every newsmagazine to which the university library subscribed so she'd be familiar with current events. She spent hours in front of the microfiche reader scanning the social columns from back issues of the newspaper, taking notes on the people whose names she saw appearing frequently.

And then there were the fashion magazines she flipped through. She had to assemble a wardrobe and it had to be just right. Day after day, she studied the inventory of Rose's Attic, trying to anticipate any event Duncan's parents might plan.

In the middle of all Rose's assembling, she realized that she needed good luggage. Matched luggage. And it couldn't be new luggage because Duncan thought she traveled.

She was agonizing over what to do when Connie breezed into the shop.

"I know that look. What are you panicking about now?"

"Luggage." Rose told her about the invitation.

"That's not what you should be worried about." Connie dumped a stack of books onto the counter where they joined Rose's. "I've got finals."

"Is it exam time already?"

"Yes, it's May and I've got to study." With both hands, Connie gestured to the stack of books. "Now, don't get me wrong. I've really, really appreciated all the overtime lately, but school has got to come first."

"Yes, of course it does." Rose stared at the books, knowing what they meant.

Connie had been working every hour she wasn't in class. Rose had been to the shop so seldom, she didn't even know who had rented prom dresses. When Connie hadn't been available and Rose had needed to leave, she'd just put the Closed sign on the door.

That wasn't a very profitable way to conduct business, but Rose had been so preoccupied first with Duncan and now the impending visit with his parents that she'd ignored the shop.

With all the credit card bills coming in, it wasn't a good idea to ignore Rose's Attic, her only source of income.

But Rose's Attic was her past; Duncan was her future. She'd worked hard establishing her shop, and she should expect to work just as hard establishing her future. Right now, she couldn't do both, but after the weekend with Duncan's parents, she'd be able to spend more time with her neglected business.

"Just work when you feel you can," Rose told Connie now, "and close the shop when you need to leave."

"Are you sure, Rose?" Connie bit her lip. "I don't feel competent enough to handle everything by myself."

"You're doing a great job." Connie wasn't about to quit, was she?

"No, I'm not." Connie dug in one of the boxes by the counter. "These are the new clothes you okayed to buy before you left for the hotel on Thursday." She pulled out a wad of multicolored silk. "I'm sorry, but I didn't notice until I'd already accepted them that this jacket is missing the top button. Maybe...maybe we could put a brooch there, or something."

They could never rent or sell it as it was, but Rose swallowed any protests. It was her fault for being gone all the time and leaving Connie unsupervised. "The jacket's so striking with all that jewel-toned silk that I probably would have ignored the missing button even if I'd known about it."

Connie's relieved face told Rose she'd said the right thing.

"And actually, I think that with the right pin it'll look even better." They both studied the jacket. It *was* gorgeous. Perhaps it would be just the right thing to take to a weekend in the country. "Would you like to hunt for a pin for it?" Rose asked.

"Yes, but first we need to check on the schedule." Connie reached over the counter and flipped open the calendar scheduling book. "The eighteenth is a prime prom night. I'll be through with finals by then, but next week is a killer. I can't be here much at all, and if the shop is closed, nobody can rent or buy dresses."

Rose looked at her. How kind of Connie to be so concerned with unimportant details like proms and Rose's livelihood. She just didn't understand that there were so many more important things. "I don't suppose you have a matched set of luggage I could borrow, do you?"

"Are you nervous?" Duncan parked his car outside the Bread Basket Foods corporate office building in an industrial area near Houston's Hobby Airport.

"Yes," Rose admitted. "I'm not sure I should be here with you. I don't know anything about advertising."

"I want you here with me," Duncan replied. "And you know more than you think. You've been our consultant on this project and you can offer a perspective to the Bread Basket honchos that I can't." He reached over and squeezed her hand. "Besides, I've missed you lately."

"Me, too." Rose swayed toward him.

He exhaled and released her hand. "Later. And that's a promise."

Belatedly, Rose saw that a woman had opened the door of the unprepossessing building and was approaching Duncan's car.

"Mr. Warren wants to meet you in building three." She pointed to another squat building in the complex.

"Thanks." Duncan waved and started the car.

Rose felt overdressed.

She wore another designer suit, this one in fire-engine red and not as pricey as the Chanel, and high-heeled dress shoes. Mark had done her hair in what he called a "corporate twist".

The woman who had directed them to the other building was wearing pilled stretch trousers and a flowered polyester overblouse.

"Duncan, maybe it would be better if I waited in the car."

He laughed. "You *are* nervous. Ah, Rose." His expression was both amused and tender. "I know this affects your future as much as mine." Lacing their fingers together, he continued, "So I want us in there, fighting together."

Future. Together. Rose clung to those words as a man Duncan introduced to her as Mr. Warren met with them in a modest conference room.

It was a room of industrial grays and whites and Rose stood out like a giant tomato. The three men with Mr. Warren eyed her like a giant tomato, too. She glanced toward Duncan, who was setting up storyboards and artwork at the front of the room and intercepted a glare from him to one of the other men.

Was he...could he possibly be jealous?

A feminine thrill went through her as she murmured noncommittal responses and primly lowered her eyes.

And then Duncan began weaving his magic. Rose was entranced and completely caught up in Duncan's vision for Bread Basket. He masterfully acknowledged the change in direction without insulting the men who made company policy.

When they balked at the singles area that had been Rose's idea, Duncan invited her to speak to them as a representative of the Village.

Rose hadn't expected to speak, though she should have anticipated Duncan's request. How could she give input if she didn't speak? But knowing he had faith in her enabled her to find the right words.

Approaching the head of the table, Rose smiled tremulously at Duncan and turned to face the four men. "The Village is a very community-oriented area. We aren't as competitive as other retail centers. The merchants support each other. We don't try to drive each other out of business. *That's* what the management of Bread Basket doesn't understand."

Rose looked for Duncan's reaction. He nodded and sat on the edge of the table, clearly indicating that Rose had the floor. Feeling bolder, she continued, elaborating on the need for a community meeting room and how providing it would help the Bread Basket store.

Rose spoke from the heart and the words were there when she needed them. She repeated virtually everything she'd told Duncan that day at the juice bar and stressed the willingness of the Village merchants to work with the Bread Basket hierarchy.

"As you can see, gentlemen," Duncan concluded, joining Rose, "the Village is willing to work with you. The question is, are you willing to work with them?" He used the silence after his remarks to gaze around the room, then gestured to her. "We'll step outside so you can discuss your options."

He looked so professionally remote that Rose couldn't tell what he thought of her speech. That changed when he closed the door firmly behind them and stepped next door into a small employee snack bar with vending machines.

"You were wonderful!" He kissed her soundly on the mouth and hugged her to him. "I *knew* you were a natural. You had them eating out of the palm of your hand. They'll probably *pay* the Village Merchants Board to hold meetings in their store!"

"Y-you really think so?" Rose thought she'd melt from the warmth of his praise.

"I *know* so." His hands gripped her shoulders. "We made a great team back there and I think—" He broke off with a lopsided smile.

"Think what?" Rose asked, her voice breathless. *Think we'd make a great team personally, as well?*

"And I think I'd like a cold drink." He reached into his pocket for change. "Want something?"

Yes, she wanted him to finish what he'd really been going to say. *Patience, Rose.* Now wasn't the time. "They've got grape soda. I haven't had grape soda in a long time."

Duncan shoved quarters into the slot and pressed the button. The can clattered through the machine.

"Is the waiting always this difficult?" She could swear there was a watermelon-size lump in her stomach.

"Always." Duncan chose a drink, as well. "But I have a good feeling about this."

"I know how much getting Bread Basket to approve the new campaign means to you and I know how much time you've spent working on it. So why didn't you warn me I'd have to speak?" Rose gingerly took a sip of her grape soda. Why did she always order items that could stain?

"You were very convincing when you spoke off the cuff that day at the gym. I didn't want you to lose that freshness."

"You took a huge risk. I might have said the wrong thing—or not have been able to say anything at all."

"I consider myself a good judge of people." Duncan took a long swallow of his drink. "I knew you wouldn't let me down."

And Rose vowed that she never, ever would.

Twenty minutes later, the Bread Basket managing directors had approved Duncan's campaign.

Rose practically floated out to the car.

"I owe a lot of this to you, Rose," an elated Duncan told her. "You were very persuasive."

Rose beamed.

He gave her an exaggerated wink and opened the door for her. "And that short skirt didn't hurt, either."

Rose tugged at her hemline as she got into the car. Duncan laughed.

"What a way to start off the weekend." Ripping off his tie, he walked around to his side of the car. "My parents are expecting us for dinner, so if I give you until four-thirty, will that be enough time for you to pack?''

Rose, who had been packed since yesterday, nodded.

Duncan shrugged out of his jacket before getting into the car. ''Perfect.'' Impulsively, he leaned across the seat and kissed her quickly.

Rose agreed. Everything was perfect.

Except that Duncan's car wouldn't start.

After fifteen frustrating minutes, he slammed the hood. ''I can't believe this.'' The smell of burnt electrical wiring hung in the heat. ''They were supposed to have fixed the problem. I certainly *paid* for them to fix the problem.'' Hands on hips, a tight-faced Duncan stared into space.

Rose told herself that it was an excellent opportunity to observe Duncan when he was angry. He was more a glarer than a yeller, but Rose never wanted to be on the receiving end of one of those cutting blue glares.

Duncan leaned over the open car door. ''I'm going to call Robert and have him come pick you up. It looks like we'll have to take your car again.'' His face softened. ''I'm sorry. But on the bright side, I might have a new car when you see me next.''

Me, too, Rose thought.

''You don't understand. I *have* to have the gray Mercedes.'' Deep breaths, Rose told herself. No, shallow breaths. She didn't want to hyperventilate.

''I'm sorry, ma'am. That car is reserved this weekend.'' The woman rental agent behind the counter looked up from her computer.

"Give that party another model Mercedes in a different color," Rose suggested, wondering why she had to think of everything herself.

"We don't have that model in another color."

"Then upgrade them. I'll pay the difference." Rose whipped out her abused credit card.

"*You* could upgrade, ma'am." The agent began typing.

"No. Gray. I need the gray one."

"I'm sorry."

"Tell them they can have any car they want. I'll pay."

The woman looked at Rose strangely. Rose didn't blame her a bit. She sounded desperate. She *was* desperate.

The woman's hand crept toward the telephone. As clearly as though the agent had spoken aloud, Rose knew she was about to call security.

"Please." Rose stayed the woman's hand. "It's just—I'm going to meet my boyfriend's parents for the first time this weekend," she blurted out. "I—I, well...that car has special, uh, memories associated with it."

"Ohhhh," the woman said in such a way that Rose knew just what memories she thought were associated with the car.

Rose's face flamed. "No, not—"

"Say no more. I understand." With a grin that made Rose's face get hotter, the woman tapped the keyboard and studied the screen. "I can let you have the car—"

"Oh, thank you."

"But it's going to cost you."

"Anything."

The agent raised an eyebrow. "Those must be some memories."

Rose thought back to the evening when Duncan had first kissed her and a smile crept across her face. "They are."

Shaking her head, the agent said, "You might change your mind when you see the total charges."

But Rose didn't. She held her breath until her credit card was approved, but she got her car.

The experience taught her a lesson. She was in over her head. As soon as the weekend was over, she'd buy a different car, but she'd buy one that she could afford.

And no more checking into the Post Oak Hotel, either. She'd continue her courses at Rice, though. They were interesting. And there was no reason she couldn't go to the symphony on occasion. So what if she didn't like the same music Duncan liked? They didn't have to agree on everything.

Feeling much more confident, Rose closed her shop, loaded the luggage she'd borrowed from Connie into the car and drove to Duncan's house.

In spite of the rocky start, the drive north to The Woodlands, a country-club community located in the piney woods less than two hours outside of Houston, was magical. Though the Friday afternoon traffic heading north was heavy, Duncan was in a celebratory mood and relayed Robert's reaction to Rose.

"He's ready to hire you," Duncan said with a laugh, "but I told him you ran your own business."

Not much lately, Rose thought. Prom season hadn't been nearly as profitable this year. Though Rose had spent the past week at the shop, it was obvious that most young women had already completed their shopping. Rose hadn't even advertised in the Village newspaper.

Apparently, her little quarter-page ads in prior years had been more effective than she'd realized.

The wedding season was just gearing up and she should already be advertising for it. She started to worry, then made herself stop.

Time enough to think about it all after the weekend.

"You know the best part about retaining the Bread Basket account?" Duncan, who was driving, turned on the cruise control and settled back.

"Either the new community meeting room or getting rid of those plastic flags and the insipid music," Rose answered.

"Yes, those things, but I've been imagining the reactions of everybody who thought Burke and Bernard had finally blown one." His smile was hard-edged. "I'll bet they'd already started working on spec ad campaigns. That'll teach them."

Retaining the Bread Basket account had obviously given Duncan a deep sense of satisfaction and he savored the victory. He talked on and on about his plans for that account and the success of other hard-fought ad campaigns. Rose was content to listen. She could listen to stories of Duncan's work all day long.

She learned a lot about the advertising business on the drive, but when they passed signs indicating the freeway exits for The Woodlands, she began to wonder about Duncan's family.

"Tell me about your parents before we get there," she asked him.

"Getting anxious?" Duncan stopped at the intersection and gave her a reassuring smile.

"A little." A lot.

"Don't be. They're nice people. My dad is a retired oil executive like nearly every other retired executive in these parts. He likes to golf, and several years ago, he and my mother moved out here to get away from the big city."

"They're not too far away," Rose commented.

"That's the idea. My sister and her family live in Houston, too, so Mom and Dad didn't want to get too far away from the grandkids." He shot her a quick look. "Present or future."

Future. Rose swallowed hard. "I didn't know you had a sister." She was probably one of the addresses in his planner, but Rose didn't know her married name.

"Yes. You remember meeting Jeanette at the symphony?"

Rose gave a horrified gasp. "She's your sister?" How could she have missed that?

"No." Duncan laughed. "But my sister, Pam, is a doctor, too. She and Jeanette went to the same medical school and practice out of the same hospital. I've known Jeanette for years."

"Oh."

"Rose." Duncan looked straight ahead. "Jeanette and I dated, and we're friends now. She's very dedicated to her career and I don't blame her." He grinned. "But I like the idea that you're jealous."

"I'm not jealous." But she was.

He grinned wider.

Rose fanned her face. "What does your mother do?"

"She's into everything. Golf, volunteering, and she's a member of about ten million organizations."

All this information subdued Rose. Duncan came from a family of superachievers. He couldn't help but compare her with them this weekend. And if she wanted that comparison to be favorable, she'd have to stay on her toes every single minute.

But she could do it. She'd been studying for days.

"This is it." Duncan turned off the two-lane road and passed through an open gate.

Yes, everything was going to be just fine.

And then Rose caught her first glimpse of the house.

CHAPTER NINE

SURROUNDED by acres of tall pine trees, the Burkes' two-story house was built next to the lake. A lush green lawn rolled down a gentle incline to a wooden pier with attached boathouse and dock.

As Duncan followed the gravel drive around to the garage, Rose saw a swimming pool and another wing of the enormous house.

She had to say something. She knew Duncan expected her to comment on the house, but all she could think about was how inadequate she felt. This was the lifestyle he was accustomed to and took for granted that she was, as well. His privileged upbringing was something she'd known but had been able to push to the back of her mind. Until now.

Loving Duncan wasn't so simple anymore.

"It's a gorgeous home." That wasn't enough. "I can see chairs on the dock. Do your parents like to sit there in the evenings?"

"And the mornings." He parked the car and turned off the engine. "It's very quiet and peaceful here. Mom's used to my jumping in the car and arriving at strange times—the middle of the day, the middle of the night. An hour listening to the water lap against the pier clears my mind."

Rose gazed through the car windows to the boat dock and wondered if an hour listening to the water would clear *her* mind.

Duncan touched her hand and she turned back to him. "Ready to go in?"

Rose drew a deep breath. "Ready."

Duncan had barely opened the trunk of the car to remove their luggage when a tall, older couple rounded the corner of the house.

Duncan's parents. His father possessed a full head of white hair, while his mother had maintained hers an attractive chocolate brown. Although both parents had blue eyes, it was his father's deep shade that Duncan had inherited.

"Duncan!" Nadine Burke lifted her cheek for a quick kiss. "And you must be Rose." She took Rose's hands in her own and gazed at her searchingly.

Rose didn't know what to say or what to do. *Please like me. I'm in love with your son.*

Whatever she saw in Rose's expression must have satisfied Duncan's mother, for she squeezed Rose's hands tightly and her lip trembled. "I'm so very glad to meet you at last," she whispered.

She saw. She understood. Rose's knees threatened to buckle.

"Farrell," Mrs. Burke said to Duncan's father, "this is Rose." As though handing him something fragile and of great value, Mrs. Burke pulled Rose's hands toward the tall man standing next to Duncan.

Farrell Burke captured Rose's hands in his own. "A lovely name, Rose. Is it by any chance short for Rosemary? Rosemary was my grandmother's name."

Rose wished with all her heart that her name was Rosemary. "No, just Rose."

"Rose," Duncan's father repeated and looked at Duncan, who had stepped back and was leaning against the car.

Rose followed the older man's gaze and caught the tender expression Duncan didn't try to hide. Her heart began beating in slow, syrupy thumps. He loved her and he was telling her now, in front of his parents. She gazed back at him, telling him she loved him, too.

Mr. Burke cleared his throat and released his hold on Rose. At the same time, Duncan stepped forward and slipped his arm around her waist, establishing Rose's position in his life for once and for all.

She wanted to cry and suspected she wasn't the only one. Nadine Burke's eyes were bright as she directed her son to show Rose to the guest room.

The first hurdle hadn't really been a hurdle at all. Why had Rose expected everything to be so difficult? Fate was on her side after all.

Fate must have thought the job was done and had taken the evening off.

Dinner was fraught with well-meaning pitfalls. Rose had relaxed as the family chitchatted on the patio while Mr. Burke grilled steaks. The heavy subjects began after they were seated around the dining table.

"Tell us about your family, Rose." Mrs. Burke began her inquisition as soon as they'd arranged napkins in their laps.

Actually "inquisition" was too harsh a word, Rose allowed. It was a perfectly natural question. "They live on a small farm in east Texas." This was completely true. However, in Texas, everyone's farm or ranch was small even when it encompassed thousands of acres.

"Oh, whereabouts?" Mr. Burke slapped a huge steak on Rose's plate.

And so it went. The Burkes and the Franklins had no friends in common as Rose knew they wouldn't, but Mrs. Burke wasn't concerned.

Rose wasn't ashamed of her background but had come prepared to feel defensive about it. She was relieved to find that Duncan's parents weren't snobbish.

"Tell us how you met," Mrs. Burke asked and it was Duncan who answered.

"I left my day planner—which has my whole life in it—at the Donahue wedding. Rose returned it, we had lunch and then we kept running into each other."

Hearing about their meetings from his point of view embarrassed Rose and she prayed he'd never discover how much planning had gone into their *chance* encounters.

"Were you at the wedding?" Mrs. Burke asked, then continued before Rose had to answer. "Did you see Stephanie's wedding dress?" She crossed her hands at her bodice. "It was *gorgeous*."

Rose liked Mrs. Burke. A lot. Mrs. Burke understood about the dress. "I did see the dress," Rose said. "It came from my shop."

"Rose owns a boutique in Rice Village," Duncan inserted, pride in his voice.

Mrs. Burke was obviously impressed with this information. "Well, the beading on that dress…it must have cost *thousands*!"

Rose opened her mouth to explain.

"No." Duncan's mother closed her eyes and waved her hands. "Don't tell me. It's none of my business."

"That's never stopped you before," Mr. Burke chided.

"Farrell!"

He sent his wife a fond look. "Do you play golf, Rose?" he asked.

"No, but I'd love to try sometime," she answered, having learned her lesson about sports.

"Rose is more of a tennis player," Duncan offered to Rose's dismay.

"Oh?" His father looked at the pair of them. "Did you bring your racquet?"

"No." Rose shook her head. Heavens, she didn't want a repeat of the tennis fiasco.

"Well, then, maybe we can sweet-talk Nadine into lending you her clubs and you and Duncan can play a few holes of golf tomorrow morning."

"I've got an errand to run tomorrow morning," Duncan said. "You'll have noticed that we drove Rose's car. Mine's in the shop."

"You go ahead and check on it, then, Duncan," said his father, "and Rose and I'll golf."

Duncan was abandoning her? To check on his *car*? Rose wasn't sure about that. Neither was she certain about golfing with Duncan's father. "Won't you be frustrated by playing with a beginner?" Rose wanted her inexperienced status to be absolutely clear to all parties.

Mr. Burke gave her an amused look. "Everyone was a beginner once."

When dinner was mercifully over, Rose jumped up to help clear the table. Carrying a dinner plate in each hand, she followed Mrs. Burke into a huge country kitchen with an attached den and enclosed sun-room. Another patio was located off a breakfast nook. Copper pots hung from the ceiling. Chocolate scented the air.

Nadine Burke handed Rose a platter with gigantic chocolate chip cookies on it. "These are Duncan's favorites." She patted Rose on the arm. "I'll give you the recipe."

Duncan's parents were being so nice to her it was almost as though they sensed Duncan and Rose's destiny. But of course they did. Fate would have seen to that. Rose shouldn't have worried.

After dessert, she and Duncan walked down to the boat dock and sat in the chairs Rose had noticed when they'd arrived. She listened to the gentle lapping of the water against the pier and tried to experience the night as Duncan might have. "Look at the stars," she said softly in wonder. "I'd forgotten how many there were."

"That's right. You grew up in the country."

"Yes." And she'd come to the city to get away from the very quiet Duncan sought. "Your parents are wonderful people," Rose said to turn the conversation away from her childhood.

"You made quite an impression on them." Duncan shifted in his chair and Rose could smell the chocolate chip cookies he'd eaten after dinner. "Maybe soon I can meet your parents."

"Maybe." Rose tried to picture Duncan visiting the farm and she couldn't. She couldn't imagine Duncan at the battered wooden breakfast table in the kitchen; she couldn't imagine Duncan milking cows or riding horses.

She couldn't imagine Duncan finding the small Texas town the least bit interesting. After all, she hadn't.

"What's the matter?" Duncan must have noticed the expression on her face. "You don't think a city boy can hold his own on the farm?"

Rose thought of all Duncan's muscles revealed by his racquetball outfit and let out a sigh. "Duncan, I think you can hold your own anywhere."

"Now that's the kind of talk I like to hear." Duncan chuckled and stretched, bringing his arm down across the back of Rose's chair.

Rather than nestling against him, she gazed at his profile. Duncan. Her one and only. Her soul mate. She shivered.

The tiny movement caught Duncan's attention and he turned his head. His hand skimmed her shoulder. "I can see the starlight in your eyes," he whispered.

That's love, Rose thought.

Duncan must have seen that, too, because he tilted his head, touching her chin so she tilted hers, as well. When his lips met hers, Rose felt the kiss all the way into the deepest corners of her heart, which thrummed with the rightness of it all.

"I feel as though I've known you forever." Duncan kissed her neck and threaded his fingers through her hair.

"Maybe you have," Rose breathed.

He pulled back to look at her. "You feel the same way?"

"Oh, yes." Rose cupped his jaw and traced the roughness with her fingers. "Right from the first."

"How did we ever find each other?"

"Fate," Rose said, and kissed him again.

*　*　*

"Well, Rose..." Mr. Burke heaved himself out of the golf cart back at the house. "I think we can safely say that golf isn't your game." He tucked the ignition key under the sun flap.

"At least I know now." Rose tried to be cheerful about the whole situation, but kept thinking of all those balls imprinted with Farrell Burke's monogram that she'd lost.

The water hazard was a water disaster. She didn't understand the point of the traps, hazards and roughs anyway. Just hitting the tiny ball into the little bitty hole was hard enough.

"That's all right." Mr. Burke put a comforting hand between Rose's shoulders. "You tried and that's all anybody can ask. Now, let's see what Nadine's fixed for lunch."

They found her in the kitchen with Duncan, who'd returned from his errand. From the way the two looked at Rose, she knew they'd been talking about her and wondered what they'd said.

"How'd the golf game go?" Duncan approached her with a kiss. Rose felt awkward about kissing him in front of his parents, but the kiss was only on the cheek after all.

"I'm not a golfer," Rose said.

He grinned. "You're so many other things, it doesn't matter."

"Yes, she told me about the Bread Basket account." Mr. Burke set the golf bags next to the wall. "Congratulations, Duncan."

"Thank you." Duncan nodded at Rose. "But Rose here deserves the credit for the idea."

"See what you can accomplish when a good woman's in your corner?" His father bent to give Nadine a noisy kiss on her cheek.

His meaning was clear. Too clear. "Oh, but the whole campaign was Duncan's idea. He spent weeks on it," an embarrassed Rose protested.

"Rose," broke in Mrs. Burke, "I've invited a few of our friends and neighbors over to meet you this evening."

Duncan whipped his head around. "Mother?"

"Now, Duncan, don't you *Mother* me. You young people are so busy these days, who knows when you'll find a free weekend to visit next?"

"Hey, wait a minute," Duncan began.

"I'll be in the study." Farrell Burke quickly escaped. Rose longed to follow.

"Mother...don't you think a party is a bit premature?" Duncan glanced uncomfortably at Rose as he spoke.

"Premature? You're thirty-two years old. I'd say it's high time!" She crossed her arms over her chest and raised her chin.

Rose hated to see them argue. "Duncan, I'd like to meet your parents' friends. It's okay." Such a last-minute gathering wouldn't be at all stressful. Why was Duncan making such a fuss?

"Then it's decided." Mrs. Burke nodded triumphantly to Rose and sat down at the kitchen desk. For the first time, Rose noticed the loose-leaf notebook in which Duncan's mother had been writing.

Duncan pulled Rose aside and asked in an undertone, "Are you sure?"

"If it pleases her, why not?"

"Because Mother doesn't know how to have a small, impromptu gathering."

At the precise moment Duncan finished speaking, Rose heard the crunch of tires on the gravel drive. Seconds later, Farrell Burke stuck his head in the room. "The caterers have arrived."

"*Mother!*"

Nadine Burke matched him blue glare for blue glare.

"C-caterers?" In Rose's world, caterers meant an important event, like a funeral or an anniversary. And, of course, weddings. In spite of herself, Rose's heart beat faster.

From the look on Duncan's face, she gathered that even in his world, caterers were used for more than a simple gathering of a few friends and neighbors.

"What have you done?" Duncan demanded.

"Everyone wants to meet Rose," his mother said in a voice that made her seem reasonable and Duncan unreasonable.

"Word spread quickly."

The caterers, arms laden, appeared at the back door. Duncan strode across the room to open it.

Rose's eyes widened at the amount of food, flowers and equipment they unloaded. Duncan merely leveled an accusing stare at his mother, who blushed.

"I think I'll go iron my jacket." Rose edged toward the door and, when no one tried to stop her, fled.

Duncan's mother wasn't planning a small, informal gathering; she was planning a major party. And Duncan was angry about it. Rose didn't have time to explore the hidden meanings of his reaction. She was thanking her good sense in packing for any possible event—except tennis.

Surveying her wardrobe, she withdrew a black blouse and trousers and the jewel-toned silk jacket. The bright colors appealed to Rose and she'd taken Connie's suggestion about using a brooch to replace the missing button. Honestly, no one would ever know.

Carrying the jacket, Rose headed back toward the kitchen in hopes of finding a utility room with an iron and ironing board. Passing through the front rooms, she saw that a huge bouquet of flowers now resided in the entryway. Rose stopped to smell the gardenias before walking on to the kitchen.

"Rose is a perfectly lovely girl. I don't know what you're waiting for." Mrs. Burke's voice carried clearly.

Rose halted in the hallway behind the kitchen.

"You're interfering again," Duncan returned.

"Again? I pride myself on *not* interfering."

"What do you call this?"

"I call *this* a nudge."

"And I call it a full-fledged push!"

"Duncan, keep your voice down."

"You should have discussed the party with me first," he said in more moderate tones.

Rose heard papers shuffling. "And give you a chance to say no?"

There was silence, then, "I'll be on the dock." Footsteps sounded and a door closed firmly, but not quite hard enough to be a slam.

Why did Duncan object to his mother's party? She wanted to asked him, then brought herself up short when she realized she'd been eavesdropping. Though unintentional, how embarrassing if she'd been caught. Waiting a moment longer, Rose stepped into a kitchen full of activity. "Mrs. Burke?"

Duncan's mother looked up, no trace of the harsh exchange with her son on her face. "Please call me Nadine, dear."

Rose didn't think she could, but she smiled anyway. "Could you show me where I can find an iron?" Rising to her feet, Nadine Burke gestured to a closed door. Rose thanked her, then said, "After I finish ironing, may I help you with anything?"

"Oh, thank you, no—but you haven't eaten lunch!" Nadine pressed her fingers to her mouth. "I completely forgot about it. Tell you what. Duncan is down at the dock. Why don't you ask him what he'd like and we'll call out for something?"

Rose nodded and left Mrs. Burke to her planning.

Though she wanted to race down to see him right that minute, Rose forced herself to gently touch up the flowing silk jacket. Duncan had told her that he liked to spend time alone on the dock to clear his thoughts, so Rose would give him a few more minutes.

On the way back to her bedroom, she noticed a squadron of cleaning people readying the house for the party this evening.

Obviously, the party was no mere whim of Mrs. Burke's. In spite of the woman's protests, Rose suspected she'd been planning this evening for days and Rose was dying to know why.

She changed out of her golf clothes into a short denim skirt, T-shirt and sandals. She'd worn these clothes before she'd met Duncan and felt comfortable in them. And she needed to feel comfortable in the hours before the guests began arriving.

Duncan didn't notice Rose's approach and she hated to disturb his solitude. Although he leaned against the wooden railing of the dock and stared at the sailboats on the lake, the set of his shoulders was tense. Something was troubling him and Rose hoped she wasn't that something.

"It's warm out here," she said to alert him of her approach.

Duncan looked over his shoulder and smiled briefly before turning back to the lake.

That wasn't a good sign.

"Your mother sent me down here to find out what you want for lunch," Rose tried again.

"I'm not hungry," Duncan said.

No, not a good sign at all.

Rose was starving and was afraid she'd be too nervous to eat later. Maybe she could find a piece of fruit or a leftover muffin from breakfast.

Joining him at the railing, she said, "You're angry with your mother."

"Yes." Then he sighed. "But she means well."

"Mothers generally do. My mother keeps thinking I'll get tired of living by myself and come home to marry one of the local boys."

"And will you?"

I certainly hope not. "No."

"You sound very sure." Duncan turned so that he was leaning on one elbow.

Rose looked him right in the eye. "I am."

Reaching out, Duncan tucked a flyaway strand of Rose's hair behind her ear. His fingers lingered as he drew them back. "And how long did it take for you to be sure?"

Rose knew he was asking something else. Something important. "I don't think certainty can be measured with time. I think that—" *when two people are right for each other* "—when something is right, you know it instantly."

She held his gaze for endless moments. The water lapped rhythmically, white sails scooted past and Duncan's smile grew.

"Rose," he said, grasping her hand, "I think you're absolutely correct." Whatever had been troubling him did no longer. Smiling widely, he simply gazed at her, then tugged on her hand. "Let's take out the paddleboat."

"What's that?" Rose was willing to go along with him, even though she hadn't eaten lunch. Time alone with Duncan was more important than food.

"I'll show you." Duncan unlocked the boathouse and revealed two boats. "This one is my dad's fishing boat. And this—" he indicated a canvas-covered lump "—is the paddleboat."

Working together, Duncan and Rose removed the protective cover and raised the canopy.

"It's like an exercise bicycle for the water." Rose looked at the two seats with pedals on the floor in front of them.

Laughing, Duncan handed her a life jacket, then had to show her how to put it on. The women he knew probably sailed on yachts every weekend and could put on a life jacket in their sleep. Rose had last worn a life jacket while canoeing at Girl Scout camp.

Duncan didn't seem to find it unusual that Rose wouldn't know how to strap on the bulky orange vest.

He was in a remarkably good mood, grinning as he stepped into the boat and held out his hand to help her. "Let's see if all those hours on the exercycle have paid off."

Minutes on the exercycle, Rose corrected mentally.

Contrary to what she feared, the afternoon was wonderful. Just being with Duncan, listening to his dreams, past and present, and seeing him relaxed was a precious gift to Rose. She absorbed everything she could about him. And what she learned reinforced the feeling of utter rightness about their relationship.

They leisurely paddled the length of the lake and back again, arriving at the Burkes' dock in the late afternoon.

"I hope your mother won't be worried about us," Rose said.

"She would have seen that we took the boat—if she's poked her head out of command central all afternoon." Duncan used his foot to keep the boat from bumping the side of the slip, then jumped out and tied the boat in place.

Rose imagined there were all sorts of special seafaring knots that she didn't know, so she didn't offer to help. Instead, she concentrated on extricating herself from the life vest.

When the canvas cover had been snapped on, Duncan walked Rose back to the house. Just before they entered, he stopped and faced her. "Do you know where my father's study is?"

Rose shook her head.

"I'll show you." Duncan looked at her intently. "Do you think you can be ready for my mother's 'small gathering' in an hour and a half?"

She could be ready in a third of that time, but didn't tell him. "Yes."

"Meet me in the study, then, in an hour and a half."

Rose's eyes widened and her mouth went dry all at once. "Okay."

Rose had been pacing in her room for twenty minutes. Her palms kept sweating and it was all she could do to remember not to wipe them on her trousers.

Duncan was meeting her in his father's study. This was important. This might be . . . It.

She paused in front of the mirror again. Mark had given her a black bow on a clip and showed her how to pull back her hair, slicking it with styling gel. Had she used too much gel? Had she used enough? Was her makeup okay? Was the jacket too much?

Rose crossed the room and entered the en suite bathroom, where she washed her hands, wringing out the washcloth and holding it to her neck. Her nerves were shot. Completely shot. She'd eaten nothing since breakfast and felt light-headed.

Her cheeks were too bright, bordering on blotchy. People would think she'd been heavy-handed with the blusher.

Duncan wanted to talk to her in his father's study. Duncan's parents had invited everyone to check Rose out. This had to be It.

Moaning, she walked to the window. From her room in the wing, she could see part of the front drive. People were already arriving and she still had another fifteen minutes before she was to meet Duncan. Unless . . . Rose tapped her watch and brought it to her ear. Was it still working?

What if Duncan was going to tell her that, in spite of his parents' open approval, he'd decided Rose just wasn't the one for him?

She was sick at the thought. Clutching her stomach, Rose sat heavily on the chintz comforter covering her bed. A few moments of deep breathing helped her regain her perspective. Duncan wasn't going to tell her any such thing. Therefore, she wouldn't think about that possibility anymore.

Rose sat there in the gathering twilight and listened as car after car approached the house, filling the driveway and parking on the grass. There must be dozens of people. No wonder Duncan had been so perturbed at his mother.

With a last deep breath, Rose stood, checked her appearance in the mirror one more time, then wobbled down the hallway to Mr. Burke's study.

She opened the door without knocking, catching Duncan by surprise. From his position, she guessed that he'd been pacing, too.

Rose barely took in the shelves of books, the leather chair and the computer before Duncan reached her. "Rose! I was afraid you weren't coming."

"It's just now seven-fifteen, isn't it?" She checked her watch at the same time Duncan checked his.

"Yes, yes, of course it is." Duncan's fingers tugged at his shirt collar. "Would you like to sit down?"

"Would I?" asked Rose.

"Oh." Duncan shoved his hands into his pockets and quickly removed them again. "I suppose there is only the one chair in here." He cleared his throat. "Rose?"

"Yes?"

Clearing his throat again, Duncan stepped forward and took her hands. His were cool. "Rose, I—" He broke off with an annoyed expression. "Everything's happened so fast..."

That he was overwhelmed by it all. Rose understood. After all, she'd had more time to get used to the idea of finding her one true love. "I know," she said. "Sometimes it takes my breath away." Inching closer to him, she smiled encouragingly.

His hands warmed and so did his expression. "We haven't known each other long, but my heart tells me time doesn't matter. I've fallen in love with you, Rose."

Rose blinked back sudden tears. "I think I've always loved you, Duncan."

He touched his forehead to hers and exhaled, squeezing her hands. With a tremulous smile, he dropped to one knee.

Rose stopped breathing.

"Rose Franklin, will you do me the honor of becoming my wife?"

CHAPTER TEN

ROSE waited for the heavenly chorus, waited for trumpets to sound. Duncan Burke, her soul mate, had just asked her to be his wife. The cosmos was perfectly aligned. Shouldn't there be trumpets?

With a soft smile, she gazed down at him. He was impossibly handsome as always, with a new, appealing hint of vulnerability in his eyes. His hand gripped hers and she could tell he was affected by the emotion of the moment. So where were the trumpets?

"Rose?" Duncan sounded uncertain, which wasn't such a bad thing for someone who was very certain of himself all the time. He could stand a few moments of uncertainty.

Rose managed another half second. Who needed trumpets anyway? "Oh, Duncan! Yes, oh, yes, I—I'd be deeply honored to be your wife."

Happiness washed over his handsome face. Standing, he squeezed her hands. "I know we haven't known each other long in days and weeks, but I don't believe waiting could possibly make me love you any more than I do now."

He said the most romantic things. Just what she needed to hear. "Oh, Duncan." Rose was conscious of not being very witty at this point, but Duncan didn't seem to notice.

He still held her hands. Shouldn't they kiss?

The thought occurred to them at the same time. Rose leaned forward the instant Duncan did. They both laughed and tilted their heads. Unfortunately, they tilted them in the same direction and bumped noses. His smile fading, Duncan masterfully cradled her head with both hands and kissed her gently, sweetly. More than once. Their engagement was sealed. Rose sighed blissfully.

"I have something for you." Duncan thrust his hand into his jacket pocket and withdrew a velvet box. "It caught my eye when I was back in town this morning." He opened the box.

Rose was blinded by a white flash as light reflected from the diamond ring. She gasped. The size of that stone would catch anyone's eye.

Duncan removed the ring, reached for her left hand and slipped the ring on the fourth finger.

"It's so big!"

"Yes, we'll have to get it sized."

But Rose had been referring to the diamond. No one she knew had a diamond that big. No one in all of Rice Village had a diamond that big. She stared at her hand and wiggled her fingers. The ring rolled from side to side, flashing and sparking rainbows, drawing attention to itself.

"We'll definitely get the ring sized, but I wanted to surprise you." He rubbed his forehead and smiled ruefully. "Not that my parents left much to surprise."

"You told your parents we were getting married?" Rose continued to stare at the ring. *No more short, unmanicured nails for me.*

"Not in those words, no. I didn't know it myself when I invited you to meet them. But something in the way I talked about you must have alerted my mother, because she's obviously planned an announcement party."

"Is that what the people are here for tonight?"

"All she's waiting for is a signal from us." Duncan picked up her hand again. "Rose, if you don't like this ring, you can select another," he offered.

Oh, dear. He thought she didn't like it. Who would not like a ring such as this? She'd get used to it in time. "It's beautiful," she said belatedly. "I'm so completely overwhelmed." Smiling, she stood on her tiptoes and kissed his cheek. "Thank you."

"You know, Rose, I feel overwhelmed, too. I never thought of myself as the impulsive type." He gazed at her tenderly. "See what you've done to me?"

He meant his words to be a compliment. She knew he did. *See what you've done to me?* Rose felt a chill slither up her back. She hadn't *done* anything, had she? She'd just put herself in his path as many times as it took for him to notice her. He had genuinely fallen in love with her. *He'd* proposed to her.

And she'd accepted. She was going to marry the young, dynamic, incredibly handsome Duncan Burke. Mrs. Duncan Burke.

As though reading her mind, Duncan crooked his arm. "And now, is the future Mrs. Duncan Burke ready to meet everyone?"

"Yes," breathed Rose, clinging to his arm. This was her fantasy, her dream. She was Cinderella and her prince had come.

He patted her hand. "It'll be fine. Everyone will love you just as much as I do."

"I hope so." More than he'd ever know.

As they walked from the study to the front room, Rose mentally reviewed everything she'd researched during the past two weeks. Judgment was about to be passed on the future Mrs. Duncan Burke. She wanted to be worthy.

As soon as Rose and Duncan stepped inside the living room, Mrs. Burke rushed over. "Oh!" She stopped and clasped her hands together. "You don't have to say anything! I can tell by your faces!"

Duncan looked down at Rose and she felt herself beam. Happy tears sprang to her eyes.

"Everyone?" Mrs. Burke clapped her hands. "I believe we have an announcement to make. Farrell? Where are you?"

"Here, Nadine." The crowd parted as Mr. Burke, wearing a hearty smile, reached out to shake his son's hand. Rose was enveloped in a great bear hug.

"Yes, yes." Mrs. Burke actually gave a little hop. "I want you all to meet Rose, who's going to be our daughter-in-law!"

A congratulatory roar swept through the assembled guests.

"Champagne!" Mr. Burke called. "The caterers iced champagne, didn't they, Nadine?"

"Of course!" She fluttered her hands at some distant waiter.

People she'd never seen before swarmed around Rose, tugging at her hand and checking out the diamond.

A dark-haired woman, not much older than Rose, raised her eyebrows. "Business must be going well," she said to Duncan. Leaning close to air kiss Rose, she whispered, "Nice catch, honey."

"I'm the lucky one." Duncan's voice rumbled firmly from above her. He'd heard. As if to emphasize his point, he drew his arm around Rose.

With a smile bordering on a smirk, the woman moved away.

"Don't mind her." Duncan spoke next to Rose's ear. "Deborah is Philip Alderman's second wife and she's never really hit it off with this crowd."

Nadine overheard. "Well, Duncan, he divorced poor Charlotte after thirty-three years to marry that social-climbing nobody." She frowned after Deborah. "We'll tolerate her for Philip's sake, but she'll *never* truly be one of us."

Social-climbing nobody. Rose swallowed uncomfortably. She watched Deborah Alderman's languid progress through the crowd. Women either barely acknowledged her with tight smiles or turned their backs and ignored her altogether.

She'll never truly be one of us. How horrible to be shunned like that. Rose wouldn't be able to bear it. She vowed to concentrate on doing and saying the right things so these people would never have cause to look down on her. She'd never be able to let up, not for a minute.

The jovial crowd moved closer. Rose found herself pressed tightly against Duncan's side but didn't mind at all. She felt safer that way. More accepted that way.

"Where will the wedding be?"

"*When* will the wedding be?"

"You'll have the reception at the club?"

"Well, where else would they have the reception but at the club?"

"Are her parents members?"

"*Who* are her people? Do we know them?"

"Where do they live?"

The questions came so fast, Rose didn't have a chance to answer any of them except the last. "East Texas," she shouted in order to be heard.

"Horrors!" A woman in a royal blue brocade trousersuit threw up her hands. "There's *nothing* in east Texas that can accommodate your wedding, child."

Rose hadn't even thought about where she'd have her wedding. In her dreams, there was always a church with stained-glass windows and pews and a big pipe organ. And, of course, she was wearing the pearl-beaded dress. The church in her little town couldn't handle the train on that dress and Rose was determined to be married in the dress of her dreams, no matter what. She sighed. The dress of her dreams and the man of her dreams. How wonderful life was.

She looked up at Duncan. He lowered his head until he was nearly touching her. Rose deliberately inhaled the scent of his freshly shaved cheek. "Let's get married in Houston," she said.

"You're sure?"

She nodded. "This is my home now."

He squeezed her hand.

"The wedding will be in Houston," Duncan announced to the room at large.

Another explosion of sound followed his words.

The blue-brocaded woman grabbed Nadine Burke's arm. "Yve's must cater the reception."

"Yve's?" Rose wondered aloud.

Blue Brocade's eyes widened. "Now, Nadine, you'll have to talk to her mother about this. Be firm. You know how these mothers of the bride want to have complete control of everything.'' She shot another wary look at Rose.

"Yve's!" A woman wearing lots of turquoise snorted. "By all means use Yve's if you want her wedding to be just like everyone else's. If I've had chicken Kiev at one wedding, I've had it at a hundred. Can't the man do anything else with chicken? She should use Wellington's.''

Blue Brocade harrumphed. ''As if we haven't all had his miniature beef Wellingtons. We get the name connection already."

"I'm sure Rose's mother and I will find someone appropriate,'' Nadine Burke murmured, unobtrusively freeing her arm.

Everything had happened so fast, Rose hadn't even thought to call her mother and father yet. They'd be so surprised. *She* was surprised. Not even in her fondest dreams had she anticipated an actual proposal this weekend. "I was just thinking of cake and punch at the reception," Rose said. "Something simple." And inexpensive.

A well of silence greeted her remarks.

Someone, maybe Duncan, closed her fingers around a fluted goblet. The champagne.

"To the future Mr. and Mrs. Duncan Burke!" Farrell raised his glass. "May all the happiness in the world be theirs.''

Rose sipped at the champagne. It was good. Really good. She drank more. It was wonderful. It warmed her. The bubbles cheered her. She drank it all.

Lowering her glass, she found the semicircle of women regarding her oddly. What was wrong?

"Well." Nadine Burke signaled a waiter. "And why shouldn't she drink?" She sent a challenging look to the women. "I've always thought it so ridiculous that the one being toasted must stand smiling foolishly while everyone else was allowed to drink."

"Hear, hear!" said Farrell.

Rose shouldn't have drunk the champagne; she remembered that now. Horrified at her gaffe, she looked at Duncan. His glass was untouched, but when his eyes met hers, he slowly and deliberately brought the glass to his lips and drained it.

Rose could feel the flush start and knew there was not one thing she could do about it. A tray appeared at her elbow and she quickly replaced her empty glass with a full one. Duncan did the same.

"And now, a toast to all you good people with thanks for your best wishes," he said.

Now she was supposed to drink and drink she did, unpleasantly aware that she and Duncan were the only ones doing so.

Perhaps this one slip could be ignored or attributed to bridal nerves. Maybe if nothing else went wrong this evening, Rose would be accepted. She'd rather die than do anything to embarrass Duncan or his parents.

The stress was giving her a headache, and wearily Rose wondered if being a part of Duncan's world would ever come naturally to her.

"Rose—it is Rose, isn't it?"

Rose nodded at the sharp-faced woman who squinted at her ring and unceremoniously dropped her hand.

"Nadine tells us you own a boutique in the Village."

"Yes." This was dangerous ground, but Rose was determined not to make her shop seem grander than it was.

"Stephanie Donahue's dress came from her shop," Nadine told the woman.

"Ohhh." The inflection in the woman's voice indicated that she was impressed. "That dress was simply stunning."

"Is that where you got your gorgeous jacket?" asked Blue Brocade. She reached out and fingered the silk.

"Actually, I did," Rose admitted shyly.

"That's funny, Joyce. You never liked that jacket when *I* wore it."

Everyone turned and stared at Deborah Alderman, who stood on the fringes of the circle. She calmly sipped her champagne.

"That's because the jacket looks better on Rose than it ever did on you," replied Joyce. "So much so that I didn't even recognize it." She smiled a lethal smile.

"Oh, I recognized it," Deborah continued to Rose's alarm. "But don't worry, you won't see me wear that jacket again. I took it to a ratty little secondhand shop in the Village after I lost the top button."

Rose felt everyone stare at her chest where a rhinestone pin substituted for the missing button.

"Oh, dear." Deborah's falsely sympathetic voice oozed into the silence. "*Yours* is missing the top button, too."

Rose wanted to die. Or disappear. Or faint. Anything to end the horror of the moment.

She wanted to be any place but where she was. If she hadn't been holding on to Duncan, her knees would have given way. She couldn't look at Duncan or his mother. She couldn't look at anyone except the malicious eyes of Deborah Alderman.

"You're out of champagne, Deborah," Duncan said, his voice faultlessly polite. "Allow me to escort you to the refreshment table." He gently patted Rose's hand and she released her grip.

Don't leave me. If you ever loved me, stay and help me through this.

But why wouldn't he leave her? He was humiliated. His fiancée had been caught wearing the cast-off clothing of a social pariah. And now he was going to question Deborah. She'd tell him about Rose's Attic, the "ratty little secondhand shop", and he'd know that Rose wasn't the sophisticate he'd thought her. And in short order, he'd know Rose was none of the things he'd thought her. He'd know that the well-dressed woman who seemed a part of his world was nothing but a fraud.

Or a social-climbing nobody.

That's what they were thinking, Rose knew. Her facade had cracked once tonight. This would shatter it. She would be exposed for what she was. Among the party guests, the speculative murmuring had already started. She could hear it.

She had to leave before she caused Duncan and his family any further embarrassment.

Rose managed to meet Nadine's puzzled eyes. "I never had a chance to call my folks," she said. "If you'll excuse me?"

"Of course."

Nadine smiled, but Rose wasn't fooled. She heard the relief in Nadine's voice. Nadine would remain publicly pleasant because she and Duncan were containing the damage. The Burkes were trying to avoid a nasty scene. Rose would help them.

Aware of everyone's eyes on her, she left the room with as much dignity as she could. She owed Duncan that much.

Rose held herself together until she was out of sight, then, pressing back sobs, she broke into a run, heedless of anyone who saw her. Once she reached her room, she closed the door and flung herself on the bed, using the pillow to muffle her sobs.

She'd come so close to achieving her dream. If only she'd had a little more time to study, a little more time to prepare for the role of Mrs. Duncan Burke. A little more time to become the knowledgeable and worldly woman Mrs. Duncan Burke should be.

The woman Duncan thought she was. The woman he loved.

And Duncan was about to discover that he was in love with a mirage. He didn't even know the true Rose. He wouldn't look twice at the true Rose. *Don't ever change,* he'd said that day they'd tried to play tennis and she'd fallen on the court.

Changing herself was all she'd been trying to do ever since she'd first seen him.

When the realization hit her, Rose felt she'd finally awakened from a long dream. That's what the past few weeks had been—a dream. She'd been dreaming to think she could pretend to be someone she wasn't for the rest of her life, even for the love of Duncan.

Oh, she'd intended to learn the ways of Duncan's world, but how many mistakes would she make along the way? How many would Duncan tolerate before her ignorance irritated him? And no matter how tolerant Duncan was, how could she endure the remarks and the sneers the way the bitter Deborah had to? How many times would the humiliating scene she'd just experienced be replayed?

She'd thought, she'd actually thought that loving him would be enough. She'd been so certain that they were right for each other that nothing else mattered. How wrong she was.

It was nearly midnight, but she couldn't stay here. She didn't belong and she didn't want to put the Burkes through the ordeal of throwing her out. She'd leave quietly. Now.

Without turning on the light, Rose dragged her suitcases, or rather, Connie's suitcases, onto the bed and began haphazardly filling them with the clothes she'd brought, including the now-hated jacket.

Since she didn't fold the clothes with care, she had to cram the suitcases shut, but before the latest bout of tears had dried on her cheeks, Rose was packed.

Her room was in the wing by the pool, but looked right out onto the front of the house. Rose opened the window and dropped her suitcases outside. Straddling the ledge, she swung her legs over. Just then, her engagement ring caught the muted moonlight.

The diamond had lost its luster, making the precious stone look cheap and fake. Like Rose. She slipped the ring from her finger, set it on the bedside table and felt a great relief. She'd never be comfortable wearing a stone that size. Yet another reason why she wasn't suited to be Mrs. Duncan Burke.

No one was about as Rose carried her suitcases to the garage. She was just congratulating herself on a successful escape when she saw that the guests' cars had blocked the driveway and hemmed in her rental car.

How was she going to get out?

The Burke house was set too far back from the road to make walking practical, especially while she was wearing dress heels. And hitchhiking on the highway in the middle of the night was out of the question.

Just then, Rose heard voices as the front door opened and a couple said their goodbyes. Stepping into the shadows of the garage, Rose watched as they wandered to their car, which was parked on the grass. They'd have no trouble getting out.

Rose knew she'd have to leave now or lurk in the garage until the people who owned the cars in the driveway left the party. Preparing to do just that, she dragged her suitcases next to the golf cart.

The golf cart! And she'd seen Mr. Burke leave the keys in it after their golf game. Rose reached inside and felt around for the sunshade. She pulled and the ignition key dropped into her hand.

Rose closed her eyes in relief. The way out would be tight, but she could do it. Quickly wedging her suitcases in the back, she hopped in and started the cart.

The engine sounded loud for such a small vehicle and Rose was afraid she'd alert the Burkes. Carefully backing the cart out of the garage, she slipped off her high-heeled shoe so she could drive more easily. Several tense moments later, Rose had driven backward between the lines of parked cars. Just as she reached the end of the driveway, the front door opened. Hoping the Burkes would attribute the sound of the motor to some maniac golfer out at this hour, Rose swerved around the cars and ducked down.

The golf cart tilted and rocked. Her shoe slid out and Rose slammed on the brakes. The stupid shoe had probably rolled under a car.

"Rose? Rose, are you out here?" A tall, dark form was silhouetted against the open doorway.

Duncan! She couldn't let him find her!

Jamming the accelerator to the floor, Rose jounced over the grass until she hit the golf-cart track and put-putted toward the clubhouse.

What if Duncan followed her? What if he thought she was stealing the golf cart?

Don't be ridiculous, Rose.

When Duncan determined Rose was really gone, he'd try to trace her through the license on the Mercedes and discover it was a rental. That ought to seal her fate as far as the Burkes were concerned.

Rose hoped by then she'd be long gone.

If she made it as far as the clubhouse, she'd leave the golf cart there and take a taxi back home. She'd have to deal with the rented Mercedes later.

Heart pounding, Rose risked looking behind her for signs of pursuit.

All she saw was a tall, lonely figure standing on the Burkes' pier.

CHAPTER ELEVEN

HOURS later, when she finally arrived home, Rose unlocked the back door, dropped the suitcases inside and walked directly through to her shop. There, she removed the pearl-beaded bridal gown from the rentals and put it on the sale rack for a price a quarter of what she could expect to get for it. Someone would be thrilled to find a bargain and Rose wouldn't have to look at the dress anymore. She knew now she'd never wear it.

Connie burst into the shop bright and early Monday morning while Rose was going over the books. "Hey, how did the weekend go?"

It was a humiliating disaster making world events pale by comparison. "Fine."

"Do you think you made a good impression on his parents?"

Rose finished writing the entry on a client's account. "I made a huge impression on his parents."

"Cool!" Connie grinned. "If his parents like you, that's half the battle."

Of course, Rose had lost the entire war, but she wasn't about to burden Connie with her troubles. Connie had finished her studies for the semester and was on her way home. To change the subject, Rose thumbed through the consignment book. "What's the status of the front racks? Time to knock down the price?"

"I guess." Connie didn't look too certain. "I'm sorry things are such a mess," she apologized. "With final exams, I didn't have time to keep current with everything." She picked up a pile of clothes, searched in vain for somewhere to put them and ended up dropping them back in the same spot.

"Don't worry about the clothes. I'm still going through that batch." And the three boxes Rose had found stacked in her office.

"Uh, the paperwork kind of stacked up, too," Connie admitted, though Rose had already discovered that. "The May consignment checks haven't been mailed."

Uh-oh. So Rose had less money in the shop's account than she thought. "Well, I would have had to sign the checks anyway."

"Yeah, that's what I figured." After a pause, Connie asked in a reluctant voice, "Do you want me to stay here and work today?"

"No, you're busy packing. Speaking of which..." Rose stepped from behind the counter and handed Connie the suitcases. "Thanks for lending me your luggage and all the long hours you've worked the past few weeks."

"I appreciated the extra pay." Connie grinned and her eyes sparkled. "We'll need it."

"*We?*" Rose raised an eyebrow.

A radiant smile transformed Connie's face. "Mark and I are getting married!"

"Married?" Connie was getting married. Connie was making the announcement that Rose should have been making.

Connie nodded, waiting for Rose's reaction.

"Oh!" Rose flung her arms around Connie, hugging her tightly. "I'm so happy for you!" Her voice broke.

"Yes, well." Flustered, Connie awkwardly patted Rose's back. "We're not getting married until next year, so you don't have to cry just yet."

Rose sniffed and grabbed for a tissue. "Sorry." She smiled through her tears. "I'm just so happy for you." *And sad for me.*

"Thanks."

They stood awkwardly, with Rose snuffling and Connie watching her warily. Rose knew she'd over-reacted and she also knew why. But explaining to Connie would ruin Connie's own happiness.

Impulsively, Rose grabbed the infamous silk jacket from the markdown rack. Only her innately frugal nature had prevented her from shredding it. "Here. Please take this as an engagement present. I know you like it."

"Rose! Oh, it's so beautiful, but I couldn't." Even so, Connie touched the jacket, the longing visible on her face.

"Yes, you can." Rose surreptitiously removed the price tag. She'd underpriced the jacket, hoping to get it out of her store.

"Are you sure?"

"Very."

Handling the jacket with far more reverence than it deserved, Connie put it into one of the empty suitcases. Standing, she gave a last, wistful glance around Rose's Attic. "I wish I could stay here and work through the summer."

"No, go on home." Rose shooed her out the door. "You need a break before the fall semester. And start planning that wedding! If there's one thing you've learned working here, it's that weddings take a lot of planning."

"Thanks, Rose."

They hugged again. Rose stood in the doorway until Connie was in her car and waved as she drove away.

But once Connie was out of sight, Rose slumped against the doorjamb. The sad fact was that she couldn't afford to pay Connie during the summer. She couldn't afford to pay anyone.

While she'd been living in a dream world, her business had turned into a nightmare. Sales were down forty percent. She'd failed to meet the deadline for the bridal advertising and prom rentals had fallen off drastically. The summer looked grim.

She needed cash. She'd had to pay the car agency extra to have the Mercedes towed. After retrieving her own car, Rose had stopped to fill the tank with gasoline. To her utter humiliation, her charge card had been refused because she'd reached her credit limit.

She wasn't broke but would have to live very frugally until the debt was paid off. That it would take years to clear didn't particularly bother her. It was, in fact, a small measure of comfort—of proof that she'd tried to make her dreams come true.

The days marched on in dreary sameness. Rose inventoried, priced and repaired clothing until she collapsed, exhausted. Only in sleep could she escape her heartache.

She was alternately afraid that Duncan would track her down and afraid that he wouldn't. She dreaded confronting him. She wanted to remember Duncan the way he'd been before Deborah Alderman had spread her poison—the expression of love on his face when he'd looked down at her as they'd accepted everyone's well-wishes.

When he discovered she was gone, Duncan would know that everything Deborah told him was true. He'd know her shop wasn't the exclusive sort frequented by high-society types except when they had clothes to unload. By now, he also knew the Mercedes didn't belong to her and probably guessed the rest. Her name wouldn't be known at any of the restaurants or appear on anyone's guest list.

Duncan Burke would soon know, if he didn't already, that Rose Franklin was a phony.

Rose knew he'd be angry and his pride would be hurt, but he'd get over her. A man like Duncan wouldn't have any trouble finding someone else. He *needed* someone else. Someone who was worthy of being Mrs. Duncan Burke.

But he'd never find anyone who loved him as much as Rose.

She knew this with the same certainty that she knew Duncan wouldn't come looking for her.

Still, each time the shop bell sounded and each time the phone rang, Rose flinched. She kept telling herself that even if he'd wanted to, he wouldn't be able to find her. She'd never mentioned the name of Rose's Attic and suspected that he wouldn't humiliate himself by asking Deborah, even if Deborah remembered the name of the "ratty little secondhand shop". Rose didn't have a private telephone line and, of course, Duncan didn't have the shop's phone number. He'd always reached her at the Post Oak Hotel and Rose wasn't ever returning there. So Duncan wouldn't run into her at the health club or at the restaurants. She supposed she'd have to miss her last class at Rice, but once she could afford it again, there was no reason she couldn't sign up for courses on other nights when Duncan wouldn't be on the campus.

No, when Duncan's anger cooled, he'd be thankful for the lucky escape.

But not Rose. Her heart was broken and would never be whole again. Yet, she regretted nothing, except the necessity of her deception, but without it, she'd never have met Duncan and would never have known true love.

It's just that love wasn't enough.

Rose held herself together fairly well. On Thursday, she had a few bad moments during the time Duncan normally played racquetball and when she should have been in class, but she didn't fall apart. She even managed to update the display window.

And then on Friday, a pamphlet delivered to her shop invited all residents and merchants of Rice Village to come by Bread Basket Foods for cake and punch on Saturday and to see the new community meeting room. The management was providing this room free of charge as a service to the community. Those interested in scheduling a meeting could call the telephone number listed below.

Rose slowly walked behind the counter and sat on the stool. The pamphlet was a glossy, four-color, professionally produced piece of advertising. It was Burke and Bernard's work, she knew. Maybe Duncan himself had actually touched this very piece of paper.

That was when she finally broke down. Clutching the slick paper to her breast, Rose sobbed, crying for her lost dreams and her lost love.

How could she bear this pain? And once it faded, what was there to look forward to? Days, weeks, months— years of sitting behind her counter waiting for customers, evaluating the castoffs of people who lived exciting lives. Rose had had her taste of excitement and look what had happened.

"I'd expected a happier reaction when you saw the flyer." The voice was deep, male and familiar. And close. "Your meeting-room idea is a reality."

She jerked her head from the counter. "Duncan!"

"Hello, Rose," he said quietly. His lips curved briefly, then sagged, as though the smile was too heavy.

Rose swiped at her eyes with a wad of tissues. She was not a pretty crier, but supposed it didn't matter. Sniffing, she stared wordlessly at him.

His blue eyes had lost their brilliance and she knew at once that she'd hurt him. She'd expected him to be angry, but she hadn't expected him to be truly hurt. "What are you doing here?" Guilt made her voice gruff.

For a moment, she didn't think he'd answer. Then, with a half smile, he carefully placed a black object on the counter between them.

Her shoe.

"I've searched the Village for the fair maiden who lost this shoe. Would you care to try it on and see if it fits?"

Rose bowed her head. "How did you find me?"

"You weren't hiding, were you?"

"I didn't think I had to." Rose wiped at a stray tear.

Duncan spread both hands on the counter and leaned forward. "You *don't* have to!"

"No, I meant that I didn't think you knew where I lived or the name of my shop."

He was silent for so long she looked up at him. She was instantly sorry she had.

Anger had burned away the hurt in his eyes. "What kind of a man do you think I am?"

"Wh-what do you mean?" She'd dreaded his anger, but seeing it directed at her was far worse than she'd imagined.

"I asked you to *marry* me!" His fingers curled into a fist. "Do you honestly believe I'd ask a woman to share my life and not know the most basic information about her?"

"Yes!" Rose lashed back. "Because that's exactly what you did!"

In the heavy silence that followed, the bell clanged as two women entered. They stopped when they saw Duncan and Rose. "Excuse me, are you open today?"

"Yes," said Rose.

"No," said Duncan.

They glared at each other.

"We'll come back at another time." The women edged out the door.

"Great!" Rose gestured after them. "Now you've scared off the only two customers I've had today."

Duncan strode over to the door and flipped the sign over so it read Closed. "Now, explain that last remark."

At the tone in his voice, Rose slumped. There was going to be a scene, a huge, hurtful scene. "I'm just not the person you think I am."

"Obviously not." Duncan stalked back over to her. "Because the woman I know wouldn't have sneaked out in the middle of the night leaving us to wonder if we should count the silver. What happened?"

What happened? "You were there. You heard what Deborah said."

"I heard her make a remark about the jacket you were wearing. Something about a button. The next thing I knew, you were gone."

Rose stared at him. "Don't you understand? *The jacket I was wearing used to belong to her!*"

As she delivered this devastating piece of information, she watched Duncan's face for the first signs of horror and revulsion. His expression remained unchanged. Obviously, the truth was so horrendous that he couldn't comprehend it.

"Not the same style, but the actual jacket," Rose emphasized. "And everyone knew it because she made sure to point out the missing button that I had replaced with a cheap rhinestone pin—which also used to belong to somebody else."

There. That ought to do it. Rose crossed her arms over her chest and waited for the explosion.

"And so you were embarrassed."

"I was *humiliated*."

"And that's why you ran away?"

Nodding, Rose closed her eyes.

"Deborah is a nasty piece of work," Duncan said quietly. "She deliberately embarrassed you. I've already spoken to my parents and they wanted me to assure you that she would not be invited to the wedding.''

''Please stop it.'' Rose sank onto the stool behind the counter. ''We both know there isn't going to be a wedding.''

''I didn't tell my parents that I found your ring.'' He reached into his pocket. ''We don't ever have to tell them.''

''Duncan.'' Rose looked at him and shook her head. ''You left with Deborah. You didn't hear what happened afterward. Everyone started whispering. I saw the look on your mother's face—she was horrified.''

''Of course she was! A guest had just insulted her future daughter-in-law!''

''No, Duncan. She'd just discovered her future daughter-in-law was a social nobody.''

His jaw worked as he visibly sought and discarded his next comments. ''At the risk of being accused of belittling your feelings,'' he said at last, ''I think you imagined these reactions. People were angry with Deborah, not you.'' He forced a smile. ''There was no need for you to run away.''

He didn't know. Miraculously, Duncan must not yet realize how she'd deceived him. It would be so easy to smile, go into his arms and let him slip that huge ring back on her finger.

But Rose couldn't do it. He may not have completely understood in this instance, but eventually he would. Rose couldn't live her life that way, dreading each time they appeared in public, wondering if this would be the occasion when she was unmasked.

"I can't do it." She was going to cry. She'd hoped if she ever had to face Duncan, she could do so with dignity. But no, she was going to blubber her way through the explanation of how she'd deceived him.

"Can't do what?"

"I can't keep pretending to be someone I'm not."

He chuckled. "Who are you pretending to be?"

"Somebody sophisticated and successful. Somebody who knows art and music and eats in expensive restaurants and wears designer clothes. Somebody who owns a Mercedes!" She covered her face with her hands.

"Oh, Rose." Duncan joined her behind the counter and put his arms around her.

It was the way he said her name. If he'd yelled or scolded or anything else but said her name as though he still loved her, Rose wouldn't have found the courage to continue.

Haltingly, she told him about studying his planner and everything that had happened after that. "You see? I've been lying to you about everything."

She expected him to turn from her in disgust. Instead, his arms tightened around her. Rose rested her head on his chest. She couldn't help it. His arms were so strong and warm and she'd thought she'd never feel them around her again.

"You've lied about *everything*?" he asked.

She nodded, no doubt smearing his shirt with makeup.

He paused, then added, "About loving me?"

"Oh, no!" She pushed back so she could see his face. "I'd never lie about that!"

He smiled down at her, his expression tender. "So you do love me?"

"Oh, yes. That's why I did everything I did."

"I love you, too, Rose." He exhaled with a long sigh. "Let's just start with that."

She was so tempted, but it would never work. Sadly, she shook her head. "You can't love me. You don't even know me."

"I know you." Duncan caressed her cheek. "I know that when I'm with you, I'm more alive than when I'm alone. For the first time, I want to share my life with someone. All the good, the bad and the ugly. All of it. I want to share it with you, Rose."

Even as her heart thrilled, she protested, "But I can't fit in your life. You take so much for granted that's new to me. And I can't even play tennis. I tried, but I just couldn't hit the ball."

For some reason, this struck Duncan as funny. A chuckle escaped. "So I'll teach you, if you want to learn."

"Stop laughing. There's more." Rose prepared to reveal the depths of her unworldliness. "I didn't like that awful piece we heard at the symphony. And I didn't get your artist friend's work at all. I thought it was stupid." There. She'd confessed.

"Well, I thought it was stupid, too," Duncan admitted. "But we'll have to disagree about *Moderno 3*. I liked it. I like modern music. You don't." He gestured around them. "See? The world didn't end because we disagreed on something."

"But, Duncan...I can't fit in with all those people your parents invited over, and if I can't be accepted by them, then I'll end up just like Deborah."

"You most certainly won't end up like Deborah!" He looked as though he wanted to shake her. "You do realize that you're accusing my parents and their friends of being snobby and shallow."

Rose was shocked at his interpretation. "I didn't mean to."

"Not only that, but it sounds suspiciously like you're ashamed of your background."

"No!" He must think she was an awful person. "I—it's only that we have different backgrounds and I didn't think you'd notice someone like me." She clapped her hands over her mouth. "I'm sorry! I didn't mean that the way it sounded."

"No, Rose." Duncan took her in his arms. "I should apologize to you."

"For what?"

"For snapping at you and for not being the person you thought I was, either."

"What do you mean?"

"There's so much illusion in advertising, so much emphasis on appearances, that I wanted to be above all that. I've prided myself on being someone who looks beneath the surface, someone who doesn't make judgments based solely on outer appearances. I value honesty—"

Rose made a sound of distress and looked away.

Duncan tilted her chin until she was forced to meet his eyes. "I value honesty," he repeated. "I've made it a policy not to take on clients if I don't believe in their product, but then look what happened with you. When you put on all the glamorous trappings, I assumed it was because they were important to *you*. I didn't realize you were doing it all because you thought *I* expected it. How could I have missed something so fundamental?''

Rose couldn't stand the anguished expression on his face. ''Because that's the only way you ever saw me.''

''No.'' Duncan shook his head. ''I should have realized what you were doing. I remember seeing you the day before we had lunch. You were in the reception area and it was so hectic…and then you were gone. No one knew who you were. I thought I'd never see you again.''

''I came back,'' she said softly.

He smiled. ''I know. Not at first, but I figured out who you were during lunch.''

''Then why didn't you recognize me at the health club?'' She'd been so annoyed that it had given her the courage to take the initiative.

''You'd changed since the first time I'd seen you and somehow I'd decided that you were just like everyone else.''

Because that's exactly what she'd tried to be. ''And so you decided I wasn't worth remembering?''

''Something like that.'' He touched her cheek briefly. ''Can you ever forgive me?''

''Forgive you? There's nothing to forgive. I *love* you,'' she said.

''Then why did you run away instead of discussing your reservations about our engagement with me?'' In his agitation, Duncan ran a hand through his thick hair, an uncharacteristic gesture that must have echoed his feelings that night. ''How do you think I felt when I discovered you were gone?''

''Angry and…then relieved.'' That was how she'd imagined he'd feel.

Duncan shook his head. "At first I was out of my mind with worry. We all were. Then I found the ring and knew you'd chosen to leave."

Rose realized she'd mishandled everything. "I thought it would be better that way. I thought that when you couldn't find me, you'd forget all about me."

"As if I could." He gazed at her a moment before asking quietly, "Weren't you ever going to contact me? I waited all week, thinking you needed time to work out whatever was bothering you."

"I was too ashamed of what I'd done," she whispered.

"Of running away? You should be."

"No—of reading your planner and...everything. I don't know how you can stand the sight of me." Tears threatened again.

"Only a person who is inherently honest would be ashamed," Duncan stated. "I'm not angry. I was hurt that you didn't trust me enough to come to me, but now I realize it was because you thought I set such store on appearances."

He was still hurt. How could she have bungled everything so badly? "No! Duncan, I was wrong. This mess is all my fault."

"Rose." Duncan reached for her hands. "We both made mistakes. I'd like us to start over."

It was more than she'd dare to hope. "I'd like that, too."

"Then promise that you'll always discuss your concerns with me. No more running away when there's a problem."

"No more running away," she echoed.

He squeezed her hands. "Good. Because the next time, I won't come looking for you."

A second chance. It was more than she deserved. "I'm awfully glad you came looking for me *this* time—and that you managed to find me."

"Why would you think I couldn't?"

"Because I'd told you I had a boutique in the Village, but I didn't tell you the name."

Duncan pointed to the glass window with the shop name painted on it. "'Rose's Attic'. With a clue like that, it wasn't hard to put two and two together. In fact, I came by one day a couple of weeks ago when I was out at the Bread Basket store, but you were gone."

"You came here?" Connie hadn't said a word.

Duncan nodded. "I wanted to see you and check on the renovations."

Rose blushed at hearing another of her lies. "You knew all along that I didn't own an exclusive, high-priced, trendy little boutique?"

"You carry one-of-a-kind vintage clothing, don't you?"

"Well, yes."

"How much more exclusive does it get?" He looked puzzled in such a thoroughly male way that it made Rose smile. "That's better. I love your smile." He reached around her to the counter and picked up her shoe. "So how about it? Will Cinderella put on her shoe?"

Rose stared at it, knowing what Duncan was asking—marveling that after everything he was *still* asking. If he believed in her and loved her enough to think she could share his life, then she ought to believe it, too.

She worked her foot out of her brown loafer. With trembling fingers, she reached for the shoe.

"Oh, no. We're going to do this right." Duncan knelt and slipped the black heel onto her foot. "A perfect fit."

Not perfect, but she'd try her best.

Standing once more, he looked down at her and asked simply, "Will you marry me?"

At the unembellished, but heartfelt proposal, Rose fell in love with Duncan all over again. None of this "do me the honor" formality. Just Duncan and Rose.

"Yes," Rose—the plain, slightly old-fashioned Rose—answered.

They stood smiling foolishly at each other, then Duncan said, "I've got your ring." He withdrew the familiar velvet box out of his pocket.

Rose braced herself for the weight of the engagement ring that he'd given her at his parents' house. Duncan hesitated, then silently slipped the ring on her finger.

They both stared. Rose tried to think of something appropriate to say.

"We'll still have to size the ring," Duncan commented, his voice flat.

I value honesty... "No." Rose took it off and handed it to him. "It'll never be the right size."

His cheeks whitened. "What do you mean?"

"I mean it's not me. It's too...cold." She gestured, at a loss for words. "Too much."

"Rose." Duncan's voice was pinched as though he was in the grip of some intense emotion.

Dropping the ring and box on the counter, he dug in his pocket and, to her surprise, snapped open a creased velvet ring box.

Reaching for her hand, Duncan slid a square-cut diamond in a white-gold filigree setting, with tiny twinkling diamonds on either side, onto her finger. This ring fitted as though made for her.

Rose gasped. "It's so beautiful!" She smiled up at him through a mist of tears. "I love it! It's an antique, isn't it?"

"Yes." There was a funny quirk to his smile. "My grandmother's. It's rather old-fashioned and I was afraid it wouldn't be enough for you."

"How could you believe—?" Rose broke off because she realized exactly why he'd believed she wouldn't like the ring. To think that if she hadn't been honest, she might never have known that he'd wanted to give it to her. "Duncan, it's perfect!"

He took her hands in his. "I give it to you with all my love and all the love this ring has seen."

Rose had never felt as happy as she did at that moment. This was the right ring for the right reasons. He really did love her—the true Rose. "Oh, Duncan!" She flung her arms around him as her tears spilled over.

"Thank you, Rose," she heard him say above her head.

She drew back. "What for?"

"For being you. For finding me. For being the right woman to wear this ring."

And as Duncan lowered his head to kiss her, Rose heard her trumpets.

EPILOGUE

On a crisp fall morning in the Rice University Chapel, Rose Franklin, radiant in a breathtaking pearl-encrusted gown with cathedral-length train, married Duncan Burke.

And they lived happily ever after.

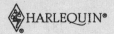

And the Winner Is...
You!

...when you pick up these great titles from our new promotion at your favorite retail outlet this June!

Diana Palmer
The Case of the Mesmerizing Boss

Betty Neels
The Convenient Wife

Annette Broadrick
Irresistible

Emma Darcy
A Wedding to Remember

Rachel Lee
Lost Warriors

Marie Ferrarella
Father Goose

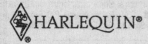